I0710680

CHASING THE STORM

SHANE KROETSCH

Chasing the Storm

Copyright © Shane Kroetsch

First edition June 2021

Pencil on Paper
Airdrie, Alberta
Canada
www.pencilonpaper.ca

ISBN 978-1-9994820-8-4 (paperback)

ISBN 978-1-9994820-9-1 (ebook)

Cover design by Francois Vaillancourt

CONTENT WARNING

This story contains scenes of graphic violence and death, gore, and gun violence.

To endings, happy or not.

ONE

Krystal rested her cheek against Evan's shoulder and held his hand on her lap. Her sandy-brown hair, tucked into a loose ponytail, cascaded over her shoulder, and scattered freckles framed her cobalt eyes. On the television across the room, an elaborate graphic lit the dim screen, proclaiming the second anniversary of the Storm. As the somber music played, her gaze fell to the regiment insignia tattooed on the inside of her wrist.

A softened media view ran the same stories over and over, showing the devastation left behind and the so-called expert's claims as to what needed to be done to ensure containment. Having experienced the worst of the event, or near enough to, Krystal had no appetite to relive it. Instead, she focused on Evan. She remembered the series of coincidences that brought them together and how sometimes good things grow out of tragedy.

Her attention returned to the screen when the broadcast changed to the situation south of the border, and the head of Homeland Security appeared on the screen. A master of dodging questions and pushing his own narrative about the terrorists responsible for the explosion, he went on about how bad things would have been if the pathogen had been released in New York City, as originally planned. He reinforced how his department would not stop until those at fault were found. Krystal did not watch the Director speaking at the podium though, it was the young man standing to his right that kept her attention. He fidgeted like he had an itch. Krystal searched for some hint in the young man's face about what was not being said.

She recited the numbers to herself before the tallies hit the screen. More than one hundred and fifty thousand bodies found from St. Catherine to Rochester. Almost forty thousand homes destroyed, some during the event, but most because of the cleanup. Combined, the US and Canadian governments spent just shy of two billion dollars to contain and rebuild. Whole industries pivoted to offer solutions. In the year after the event, the unemployment rate in the more populated areas affected was at an all-time low.

The vaccine arrived six months after dispersal, but between the reinstatement of quarantine, medical checks, and the lifespan of the infected, the infection itself had nearly burned itself out by then. Flare-ups tended to be small and simple to extinguish. Regardless of the quoted numbers, concerns over how bad it could have been or what it would look like if a second wave hit were never far behind. Despite the government's best efforts, the infection found its way to the UK and Asia. Krystal understood the instinct to go home, but not how some could ignore the consequences. Thankfully, enough had been learned by that point to keep the outbreaks easily contained. For the most part, anyway.

The newscast brought up theories of how the Russians

were to blame, or aliens from Mars. They failed to give any legitimate indication of where the pathogen was created, or mention the soldiers in black and the unmarked planes seeding the clouds to build the storm's intensity. Like many things, the answers given were not answers at all.

When the camera refocused on the newscasters, a blonde flashed her perfect teeth as she recapped the weather forecast. Her partner, with chiseled features and a wild patterned tie, collected his papers and tapped them against the desk to even them out.

"Sunrise tomorrow is at seven-seventeen and sunset is at four forty-eight. Be sure to tune in for our live coverage of the remembrance ceremonies. Have a safe evening, everyone."

Evan pointed the remote at the TV and lowered the volume as the newscast went to commercial. "That's enough of that."

Krystal closed her eyes and nuzzled into Evan's neck. "Finally."

"Sorry, I know it's not your thing."

"It's okay."

Evan turned and kissed Krystal on her forehead. "You want a beer?"

Krystal pushed his arm away and sat up. "Stay, I'll get them."

Reaching out for the handle of the fridge, she paused at a buzz in her pocket. When she pulled her phone out, a text from Clint lit the screen. Krystal swiped to enter her password, then pressed the icon to call. "What's up?"

"Hey, Cuz. We still on for eight?"

"Of course."

"Good. Everything else all right?"

"Suppose so. It'll be better when this anniversary bullshit is over."

Clint grunted. "I hear ya."

"Hey, Jacob and Mati were over today. They said to say hi."

Clint did not respond right away. "They're still together?" His question lacked emotion.

"Well, not together, together. Evan says it was never like that."

"Yeah, that's what Jacob used to say. I didn't get it at the time." He cleared the tremble from his throat. "Anyway, guess I'll see you in the AM."

"Sounds good."

Krystal opened the fridge, pinched the necks of two bottles in her fingers, and walked them back into the living room.

TWO

Krystal pulled her car into the far end of the gas station parking lot. A shiny Dodge quad-cab was parked at a lousy angle across three stalls. Jacked up on oversized black rims, the once aggressive tire treads were well-worn from use, the truck's license plate announced 'ZMBHNTR'. Clint leaned against the bed with a cigarette smoldering in one hand. Large, mirrored glasses covered his eyes, protecting them from the early morning glare. He scratched his unkempt beard as Krystal approached.

She set two bags in the bed of the truck, a backpack with multiple compartments and a bedroll tied to the bottom, and a square duffle covered in pink camouflage. "Mornin'."

Clint nodded and blew out a thin stream of smoke. "The fuck is that?"

"What, the bag?"

"Yeah, the bag. What the hell else would I be talkin' about?"

Krystal shrugged and looked off across the parking lot. "It's from Evan. He's trying."

Clint laughed. "That's trying?"

"Knock it off. He's a good guy."

"If you say so."

Krystal held out a ring of keys. "Trade?"

Clint took the keys and held out a ring of his own. "I'm past due on the oil change. Take it a little easy if you can."

Krystal glanced sidelong at Clint as she headed back to her car. "You need to take better care of your shit. Especially when it's responsible for getting me to and from the middle of nowhere in one piece." She popped the trunk and removed a rifle case and a plastic cooler with a snap-on lid and a skull painted on the side. With the rifle over her shoulder, she hefted the packed cooler and walked them to the truck. "Is that our group?"

Clint nodded toward the convenience store and the group milling about beside the ice machine. "They sure do look like a bunch of insurance salesmen, don't they?"

One of their customers leaned against the building with a foot flat on the brick and a big, dumb grin on his face. Two others stood to the side, one tall with broad shoulders and hands in his pockets and one shorter with thinning hair and thick glasses riding low on his face. Each donned unique combinations of printed camouflage, safety orange, and the best hiking boots money could buy. All were new, without a single scuff on them.

"Names?"

Clint spat and ran a hand down his beard. "Christ, I don't remember."

Krystal frowned. "Great."

"Hey, I'm the equipment guy and take the money. You're the personality."

"I guess. Did you at least get the waivers signed?"

"Yeah, of course."

"They've got their tags?"

"Yup. Two apiece."

"Really? Seems ambitious."

"A little? The younger one was all proud of going to the range and learning how to shoot."

"Gotta love the newbies." She shielded her eyes against the sun and looked at Clint. "What are you up to now?"

Clint focused on the ground and shrugged. "Kids want me to take 'em toy shopping today. Erica says no because Christmas is coming up and all, but we'll see."

"How's that going, anyway?"

Clint took a long drag from his cigarette. He exhaled to one side. "It ain't really."

Krystal frowned. "Sorry."

"It is what it is." Clint shook the keys in his hand. "You should get movin'. Daylight's a-wastin'."

"Suppose so. Give the kids a hug for me. Tell them Auntie will have something special for them when she gets back."

"What, like a deer skull with a bullet through the forehead?"

"Ass."

Clint let out a sharp laugh. "Hey, might take some of the heat off me."

"You'd like that, wouldn't you?"

"Yeah, I would."

Krystal shook her head and a smile fought at the corners of her lips. "All right, I better get on with it."

Clint tossed his cigarette butt on the gravel and walked to Krystal's car. "Have fun."

Krystal zipped her vest and set off toward the convenience store. The three men fell silent as she approached. She stopped a few steps from them with her feet wide. "Gentlemen."

At the far end, the short one pushed his glasses up his nose and squinted. "Are you with…" He motioned to the truck.

Krystal nodded. "That's me."

The short man frowned. "Oh. Umm. I thought the guy with the beard…"

Krystal tilted her head ever so slightly. "The beard has other things to worry about. My track record is far better anyway." She took one step forward and extended her balled fist. "Krystal Atherton."

The short man made a false start before reaching his hand out and bumping it against Krystal's. "Darby. Darby Snyder."

Krystal turned to the one in the middle with enough product in his hair to fuel a small city for a day. He seemed young, his eyes wide and optimistic. While sticking out his fist, he gave her a little wink. "Ellery Bindra."

Krystal bumped his knuckles and moved on to tall, dark, and handsome. Eyes, bright and icy blue, locked onto hers, and his clean shave showed off his sharp cheekbones when he smiled. "Johnathan Haywood."

"Nice to meet you. All of you." She forced herself to step back. "Right, drop your bags in the bed of the truck. I'll secure the rifles. Before we head out, be sure you leave your license plate number with Ranjit at the gas station, so you don't get towed. While you're there, grab some road snacks and hit the toilet if you haven't already. We've got a bit of a drive ahead of us, and to stay on schedule, we won't be stopping."

Johnathan and Ellery nodded while Darby just stared. Krystal clapped her hands. "Go, go, go." She stepped to one side and held out an arm to guide their way.

Droning tires on cold pavement filled the cabin with white noise. Ellery joked and talked at, more than talked with, Johnathan in the back seat. Darby sat close to the side window and watched the scenery pass by. Krystal almost managed to zone them out when Ellery knocked on the plexiglass partition separating the front and back seats. He spoke loud and slow. "How long until we arrive?"

Krystal pushed a button on the dash to silence the radio, and a two-level tone rang out. "You don't need to shout."

"Oh." Ellery's voice sounded through the stereo speakers.

"We're still another hour or so out. Sit back and relax."

Johnathan leaned forward. "Where are we going, exactly?"

"We're going to the biggest bucks you're ever going to see. That's all you need to worry about."

Johnathan shrugged and sat back.

Krystal checked the rearview mirror. "We worked hard to get access. The quieter we keep it, the longer it pays off, that's all. It's all above board."

She focused back on the road. "I heard you guys booked this trip a while ago. Anything to do with the anniversary?"

Johnathan nodded. "It was my idea. It's something that's been on my mind. A way to recognize what happened, maybe." He leaned against the door and watched the shoulder of the road drift past. "I lost my parents, my brother, too. They never found his body, or it wasn't identified. I hate to think if he turned, I mean, what he might have done…"

Krystal pinched her lips into a tight line and nodded. She looked to the corner of the mirror. "What about you, Darby?"

Darby stared out the side window. His face was drawn. "I

lived in Fort Eerie when it happened. Did you hear the story about the kid that killed his father but let his mother and sister live?

"Shit, that was your family?"

Darby shook his head. "No, our neighbors down the block. The army burned the house down after what they found inside. We went back once the quarantine lifted. Half the neighborhood was ash. We couldn't stay. It was too much." He faced forward. "I know we didn't go very far, but it was important for us to put some distance between. My wife wants us to move back to Gander. No infection out on the island and all that. This could be my last chance to take back some of what's been lost."

Ellery smiled through straight white teeth when his eyes met Krystal's in the rearview mirror. "I just wanted to be a part of something special, you know? Shit, I was barely out of high school when the storm hit. People I knew got sick, distant relatives and what-not. Life is short, might as well make it an adventure."

Quiet settled over the truck. Krystal reached out for her phone to start the music again, but Johnathan interrupted.

"What about you?"

Krystal slowly withdrew her hand and rested it on the wheel. "We all lost people. We all saw things we wish we hadn't. That's all that needs to be said."

She pressed a button on the dash, then took up her phone and scrolled through her playlist. A rolling drumbeat echoed through the passenger compartment. Krystal set one hand on top of the steering wheel and focused straight along the road.

———

Half an hour into a bouncing ride down a narrow, rutted dirt path, Krystal spotted the familiar strand of yellow nylon ribbon tied to a tree branch. She brought the truck to a stop and jumped out, then hopped across a shallow ditch. She came to a roughshod gate, untied a weathered coil of rope from the post, and pulled the gate open. After driving the truck to the other side, Krystal reversed her efforts. Branches grazed the side mirrors and scraped the windows as they eased through the dense grouping of spruce and birch trees. Soon, the path opened and turned from dirt to jagged gravel. A river carved a clearing through the forest, and the thundering pressure of flowing water radiated from the ground.

Krystal navigated the truck near the bank and angled it into a loose grouping of low bushes. She leaned forward on the wheel and pressed the speaker button on the dash. "Take a few minutes to stretch your legs. I'll let you know when it's time to go." She turned to the group. "Don't go far. Bears should be hibernating, but that's not the only thing out there that might be looking for a snack."

Ellery grinned. "So, you're saying I look tasty?"

Krystal faced forward before she rolled her eyes. She released the button, then cut the engine.

THREE

In the darkness, a red light changed to green. A heavy door, flush with the wall, popped out on its hinges with a release of pressure. Fluorescent lights hanging from the open ceiling flickered to life.

A man walked through the opening, holding a large aluminum travel case. A pair of wireless headphones draped over his neck, and a low-profile respirator hung below them. Fast-paced music added steady background noise to the otherwise quiet space.

Rubber soles squeaked on the polished concrete as he turned right and walked past a cargo elevator sunk deep into the wall. Across the open floor, two others faced it. Each had a standard door beside, and to their left, a pair of power jacks sat parked on their chargers. He stopped in front of a double barred steel door. Windows, filled with wired security glass, were set in the cinderblock wall on either side.

"Jesus, Isaac. Could have said something about how frickin' cold it is down here."

While fastening the top two buttons of his dark blue work

shirt, the man's arm brushed a plastic name badge on his chest. Looking down, he turned it face up. 'Wagner' was engraved in a stylish font.

"Oh shit."

He looked back through the heavy open door and scanned the ceiling for cameras. Fishing a hand through the button closure, he pulled the magnetic backing out, then dropped the badge in his shirt pocket.

The man reached into his cargo shorts and took out a phone. Swiping to the last screen, he tapped on a blank icon, the display pinged, and went dark. Flipping the phone to his opposite hand, he held it out to a discreet circular panel sunk into the cinderblock wall. A ring of green light surrounded the circle, and with a click, one side of the barred door released.

Stashing his phone away, he took a pair of black gloves from his back pocket. The smell of recently tanned cowhide helped push away the heaviness of sweat and urine in the air. He flexed his hands to stretch the leather out, then secured the respirator over his face.

"Okay, let's do this."

The man lifted the travel case from the floor, pushed the door open with one foot, and proceeded through. Another cinderblock wall split the room in half. On either side of it, two rows of steel cages stretched the length of the space. Each had fork-lift slots in the base and were no more than chest height. They looked like something one would find at a zoo to transport big cats. On the right side, banks of rectangular light fixtures cast little more than a dim glow. The man positioned himself on the left side, where the fluorescents flooded the area with harsh light.

He set the case on a three-tier stainless steel cart that had a yellow biohazard disposal hanging from one end. The metal clasps on the case snapped back, and he spread the top wide. Open compartments held bundles of individually wrapped syringes and needles, plastic gloves, and spare masks. The man removed a zippered hard-shell fabric case from the bottom and set it on the cart. Next, he brought out three short rods, two white and one with a black rubber handle. Laying them out to ensure the correct order, he threaded them together into a single length.

With a tremor in his hand, he unzipped the fabric case and flipped the top back. A wide elastic band held a row of slim plastic syringes filled with murky liquid. He counted twelve per side. Each had a needle already affixed.

The man shook out his free hand and stretched his neck. "Pull yourself together, you got this."

He pushed out a long, slow breath, then adjusted his headphones over his ears. He pinched the bottom of one syringe and slipped it from the case. Pointing the needle away from himself, he threaded it onto the jab stick. With the rod held well out in front of him, he stepped toward the row of cages.

The man stopped at the first cell and moved the cart ahead of him, parking it in the middle of the aisle. Standing in front of the cage, but two steps back, he paused with his arms held out from his sides. The man's breath came short and shallow. He stared at a bundle of gray fabric balled up at the back of the cage. Old stains mixed with new, and threads unraveled at the edges. It could have been a pile of dirty laundry, but the man knew better. He pushed out a sharp exhale and stretched one foot toward the cage.

It required both hands for him to guide the needle through the bars. He settled his stance, then counted down from three in his head before thrusting out. The tip of the needle plunged deep into the blankets for a split second before being yanked back. The pile of fabric shifted, but soon settled. Holding the stick to the light, the man confirmed the syringe was empty.

"Huh, that wasn't bad."

He unscrewed the needle and dropped it through the top of the yellow disposal, then took another syringe from the case and moved on to the second cage.

By the end of the first row, he had the process down to seconds. Add a fresh syringe, stick, dispose, and repeat. By halfway back in the second row, his shoulders had relaxed, and his head bobbed to the constant stream of music. He discarded the twentieth empty syringe with his back to the cages and threaded on the next. When he turned around, he stumbled and nearly dropped the stick.

Deep in the shadows of the cage, glassy eyes peered through dark, stringy hair.

"Help me."

The man froze in place.

As the blanket fell away, a sullen face emerged. Makeup smeared across gaunt cheeks. The woman's chin trembled. "Please…help me."

"Shit." The man shifted his weight from foot to foot. He stole a brief glance along the remaining cages. "Shit, shit, shit."

Crawling forward on her hands, the woman repeated her plea. "Help me."

The man did not respond.

She strained to raise her voice. "Help me. *Please.*"

The man's eyes widened, and his hand shook.

Stained fingers wrapped around the mesh of the cage door, and the woman bared yellow teeth. *"Fucking help me, you fucking—"*

The needle sunk deep into the muscle above her collarbone. The woman screamed and collapsed. Sobbing, she pulled the tattered blanket over her head and pushed back to the far corner of the cage.

As the man stepped aside and fought to unscrew the syringe, a dark form slammed against the front of cage twenty-two. The man flinched. The used syringe slipped from his fingers. He lunged to catch it but missed. With empty hands held out from his sides, he looked down at the needlepoint stuck deep into his shoe, like a javelin in soft earth. He exhaled an inaudible noise and tensed every muscle in his body. His face lost color as panic filled his eyes.

The commotion inside the twenty-second cage continued. Thick, grease-stained fingers shook the door, and a deep voice snarled threats, but none of it registered. The man's throat had seized. Under the respirator, he licked his lips, but his tongue was dry. Bringing one hand in front of him, he bent down.

"Holy…fucking…shit."

His fingers spread wide around the syringe, then snapped like a mousetrap and snatched it from his shoe.

The man dropped to the floor. He kicked his shoe off and peeled his sock down. With one hand on his heel and one around his toes, he pulled his foot close to his face. A tiny red spot showed between the long bones on the top of his foot. He rubbed at it with this thumb. When the mark did not return, he released the burning air from his lungs. A choking laugh escaped, but he held it in when it threatened to change to crying. Letting his foot drop, he leaned forward and covered his eyes with his hands. After rubbing his face, a smile tugged at his lips.

The figure fighting against the cage door continued to spit and curse. The man stood to face the cell with his arms wide.

His smirk turned to a sneer, and he launched forward and slammed the flat of his shoed foot against the cage. As he made contact, he screamed.

"Shut the fuck up."

Jolting back, the figure in the cage fell silent, save for their labored breathing.

The man bent down to retrieve his abandoned sock and shoe. He took one brief look around. "Shit." Tears built up in the corners of his eyes. "Just, shit."

Turning on his bare heel, he ran. Squeak, slap. Squeak, slap. He hurled himself through the steel barred door, leaving it wide open. Pulling on the heavy door to the upper level, the man disappeared as it suctioned shut.

FOUR

Dense clouds settled, and the temperature trailed off as the group continued upstream. The wind blasted Krystal's face a deep shade of pink, her ponytail flipped behind like a flag in a storm. The men hunched low with their faces covered. Each had a rifle case at their back, along with a tall pack topped with a sleeping bag. Ellery held his hood taught to minimize the damage to his quaff.

Near a break in the forest, an ancient, uprooted tree laid across a stretch of rough gravel with the narrow end of the trunk dipping into the water. Krystal sidled up to it, set the cooler down, and rested her hand on a crooked root.

Ellery huffed clouds of warm air when he came up to Krystal. He squinted his eyes and looked back the way they came. "How much longer?"

Krystal stretched out her frozen cheeks. "Not much longer." She pointed into the trees. "We head in here."

"Hopefully, it will cut the wind a little."

Krystal brushed her hands together, then bent down to retrieve the cooler. "We're about to find out."

Twenty minutes in, the group came to a clearing of sorts. In the middle of the widest part, a mound of coal and ash filled a crude stone ring. Nearby, four posts held a sloped roof, covering benches along two sides and a plate metal firebox in the middle. Tucked at the back of the clearing was little more than a tall shed. A single padlocked door sat off the narrow porch with a hazy window built into the wall next to it. A black stove pipe stuck through the north slope of the peak, and solar panels lined the south.

Johnathan motioned toward the structure. "What's that?"

"That's home." Krystal set her bags down. "The cots are set up and ready for you. I'm sure it's more basic than you're used to, but there are lights and heat. You'll be comfortable enough."

Ellery made a face. "Doesn't look big enough for four."

"That's perfect then, because it only needs to hold three." Krystal walked across the clearing to a bent tree and planted one boot against the trunk. Reaching for a low branch, she hoisted herself to grab a small canvas sack nestled higher up. It dropped to the ground, then Krystal landed next to it. Rummaging in the sack, she found a ring with a bullet casing keychain, holding a single key. "Heads up." She tossed it to Johnathan. He flinched but snatched the keyring out of the air.

Krystal shouldered her bags. "Go get settled, then we'll start a fire and get something warm to eat."

"Wait, where are you going?"

Krystal glanced over her shoulder. "I have private accommodations."

Ellery smirked. "Damn, it probably has a real bed and Wi-Fi."

Ignoring the comment, Krystal walked off into the trees.

———

The group sat with full stomachs and heavy eyes, watching the fire flicker and crack. The world around them was quiet and still. Warmth from the fire wrapped around them like a blanket.

Darby yawned and rested his chin on a closed fist. Ellery pulled his hood over his head and leaned back with his arms crossed. Johnathan sat forward but lifted his face to the sky.

"Krystal?"

"What's up?"

Johnathan focused back on the fire. "How long have you been doing this?"

"Doing what?"

"Hunting. Bringing people out here."

"I've been hunting since I was a kid. This is the second season we've been coming here."

"Did you go somewhere else before?"

"We only got serious about it after the lights came back. At first, it was a friends and family only type of thing. We bounced around to different spots, calling in a bunch of favors. Negotiations to get access here took a while. It was a weird time."

"This wasn't what you did for a living? You know…"

"In the before times? No."

"What did you do before?"

"Do we really need to do this?"

Johnathan shrugged. "Not if you don't want to, I guess."

"Hey," Ellery raised a pointed finger, "we told you why we're out here. Now, it's your turn, right?"

Krystal frowned, focusing on the fire while the others focused on her.

"Fine." She took a sip from the insulated mug held at her lap. "I worked warehouse distribution in Toronto for a few years before the lights went out. On the side, I was in the Reserves. Military sort of runs in the family." Krystal cleared her throat. "It took the people in charge a little too long to figure out how bad the situation was, and it took even longer to get mobilized. We landed just outside of what the containment zone was at that time. Basically, we formed a giant net and squeezed our way to the border. Sundown to sunup, for days. We had to learn how to find the infected and how to avoid getting sick as we went. Lost a few too many before that one got sorted."

"Near the end, I pulled some strings to make sure I was in the group that moved on Fort Erie. My cousin Clint, the beard, lived on the edge of town."

Darby sat forward, picking at the dirt under his fingernails as his eyes darted around the space.

Krystal took another sip but went on without acknowledging Darby or pointing out the connection to his hometown. "I don't remember breathing as I walked up the steps and knocked on the door, not until it opened. We lost my cousin Davie, Clint's brother. The rest of the family was okay, or as okay as they could be.

"I won't ever forget the look in Clint's eyes—the defeat. Don't get me wrong, he's not perfect, but he's a good guy. Seeing him so broken, well, it broke me too. So, when things were over, we both ended up drifting away from the lives we had before." Krystal wiped at her nose. "In some ways, whether we wanted to or not."

Johnathan lowered his eyes and shook his head. "That couldn't have been easy."

"It really wasn't." As Krystal drew in a deep breath, cool, humid air prickled her lungs, and she coughed into her arm.

A heavy silence fell over the group as they refocused on the fire.

"Anyway. Here's to the before times." She raised her mug in salute, then drained it and stood. "I'm done. See you all in the morning."

FIVE

Ray tilted the last of the pale amber liquid past his lips. He held the crystal rocks glass out to consider it as warmth spread across his face. When he set it down, melting spheres of ice clinked together.

"Been a long day, Cal. Can't think of a better way to end it."

Across from Ray, Callen sat rigid in his chair with his hands hanging over the plush armrests. The soft, yellow glow from the small lamps spread across the room, casting shadows over his stern face. He stared out the floor to ceiling windows at the erratic choreography of falling snow beyond.

Ray reached up to take out a skin-toned earpiece and let the thin wire hang down the front of his shirt. A leather bracelet sewn with colorful beads in an intricate pattern slid down his wrist when he took the stopper from a hand-blown liquor bottle on the narrow table beside him. "You sure you don't want any?"

Callen pushed out his lower lip and shook his head.

Ray guided his hand to the bottle and poured himself a

generous portion. He replaced the stopper on the second try, then leaned back in the chair with his glass held up. His smile came slow and demure. "Hope you don't mind if I partake?"

"Kind of you to ask, but you're good."

Ray ran a hand over his hair, straight and black, with strands of wiry silver along the sides. "You know, I don't think I've ever seen you drink before."

Callen did not break his attention from the windows. "Haven't touched the stuff in a couple years. Doesn't do anything for me anymore."

"Fair enough." Ray sipped at the glass. "I got rid of it all when my daughter was born. But then, I'm not at home, and if a drink or two helps me sleep through the night, so be it."

Callen shared no response.

Ray took another drink. "First of the guests still in around noon?"

"As far as I've heard."

"Are we getting another delivery tomorrow?"

"No, the last arrived this afternoon. They stacked 'em deep. All prepped and ready to go."

"Good. Don't want to have to deal with that bullshit right before we open the doors."

Callen nodded.

Ray sighed and rubbed at his temples. "How long you been here now?"

"Little over a year, I think."

"Sounds about right. Guess you were here pretty much from the start."

"Close enough to."

"Do you…I don't know, enjoy this?"

Callen drew in a deep breath and turned to Ray for the first time. "Not the way I'd put it. It's a job."

"Then why do you stay? I know the money is good. It's the rest of it that I'm not so sure of."

Callen's focus faded. "Everyone gets to decide what lines they cross and what ones they don't."

Ray lowered his eyes and pursed his lips. He let the long list of regrets and not leaving when he had the chance take space for only a moment. After giving the drink in his hand a thoughtful glance, he set it down. "This is true."

He gripped the arms of the chair to push himself up, but he stopped mid-movement as a dull noise reverberated through the room. Ray and Callen locked eyes.

"The hell—"

Another thud shook the walls, and the lights went out. Callen jumped from his chair and sprinted for the stairs before Ray could finish his question. Dropping to the first step, he popped the snap on his holster and drew a gun from his side. Callen descended two or three steps at a time, then slammed into the door at the bottom. He swore to himself. No electricity meant the sensors were no longer working. Staggering back, he fished a heavy key from his pocket, unlocked the door, and pushed through.

Callen pumped his legs, pushing along a wide corridor as worried glances from the staff setting up the dining area on the main level flashed past. Halfway down, he stopped at an exterior door, slipped in his key, and burst outside.

Cold air stole his breath as he ran through ankle-deep snow toward the back of the building. Uncountable stars and the waning gibbous moon gave enough light to guide his path, though he was not focusing on the ground in front of him. To the north, a flurry of headlights bounced as snowmobile engines undulated and screamed their retreat.

At the tree line, a low building with a string of small

garage doors cracked open in a flash of orange. The roof at one end bulged, then collapsed. With the explosion ringing in his ears, Callen ran on.

Stopping well out from the rear of the main building, he saw the once tidy box that encased the mechanical area now laid broken and twisted. Smoke billowed as the fire grew, and pockets of steam sprung from the ground as chunks of red-hot metal melted the snow. He traced the trail of jagged debris until his eyes locked onto the corner of a chain-link enclosure set back from the building.

The outermost post bent to the point of cracking, and pieces of charred equipment laid close by. Larger pieces of the mechanical cage had blasted through the fence like knife blades, leaving sections of chain-link coiling in on themselves. Callen stared past the void into the darkness. He held his breath, so it would not obscure his vision, and waited.

Sensing the first hint of motion in the flickering firelight, he spun away. He raced along his own tracks, retreating to the open door as links of metal fencing clinked together behind him.

Callen fought against the ache in his legs until he reached the entrance. Pulling the door shut behind him, he collapsed against the wall and closed his eyes, flashes of pressure pounding at his temples. When the pain eased, he righted himself, sat with his forearms balanced on his knees, and hung his head low.

"Cal?"

Callen coughed and looked up, still straining for air.

Ray stood with one arm loose at his side, the other held his phone's flashlight pointed at the ground. "What's going on?"

Callen cleared his throat, then coughed again. "They blew the solar generators. The second pen's been breached."

"Br…breached? What do you mean?"

"I mean, there's a big fucking hole in the fence."

Ray's eyes widened. "But…"

"Yeah."

Ray covered his gaping mouth.

Callen looked to the floor. "Time to call the boss."

Ray faced the empty corridor. "When does the security transport arrive?"

"We're not going hunting, Ray. Besides, they don't land until tomorrow morning with the rest of the staff." Callen sighed and stood on sore legs. "They won't get far. We'll contain it. Call Kennington."

Ray let the words sink in, then stomped down the corridor with a bow-legged gait. "Fuck." He paused at the door to the lobby, then looked back with a red face and shouted. "I'm too old for this shit, Cal." The door slammed shut behind him.

Callen lowered his head and ran a hand over his face. "Me too, Ray."

SIX

"Good morning."

Krystal looked up as the door of the camp stove creaked shut. "Morning." She set her hands on her knees and pushed herself up to stand. "How'd your first night go?"

Johnathan shrugged. "Well enough, once I got used to Darby snoring."

"Could be worse then."

He nodded. "What do ya have going on here?"

"Oatmeal and some frozen berries. It'll give you guys a good start."

"Nice. Thank you."

"No worries." Krystal brushed her hands together. "It's part of the package."

"Right, of course."

The cabin door pushed open. Ellery yawned and stepped across the threshold while stretching his arms wide. Noticing Krystal and Johnathan watching him, he curled his lips into a smile and waved. Footsteps on the cold earth echoed around the clearing as he neared. "Shit, it's cold out here."

Krystal stepped back and motioned to the stove. "Come warm up."

Ellery stuck his hands deep in his pockets. "I'm good." He scanned the forest and drew in a cold breath. "This is amazing. Must be nice to spend so much time out here."

"It has benefits, for sure."

"You've got a pretty nice setup. Business must be good."

Krystal shook her head. "Not bad. It pays the bills and puts a little food on the table, but if you think anyone's getting rich, you're wrong. Transportation, upkeep, it all adds up."

"You must enjoy it, though, right?"

"For the most part, I do."

The cabin door slammed shut. Darby shuffled out into the clearing with his arms crossed and a scowl on his face.

Krystal sighed. "Oh, good." She turned to the stove and lifted the pot of cooking oats with a towel draped over the handle. "Time for breakfast."

SEVEN

Ray leaned forward with cupped hands over his mouth and the tips of his fingers resting on the end of his nose. Battery-powered lanterns on either end of his desk cast faint light over the room.

"How bad is it?"

A scowling man in blue coveralls leaned against the open door frame with his arms crossed. "It's bad."

"Can you fix it?"

"No, I can't fucking fix it. Pieces of very expensive, very specific components are scattered everywhere. How the fuck do you expect me to fix it?"

"Hey." Callen stepped forward from the back wall of the office. "Dial it back a little, Remo."

"Dial it back? Why do I have to be the one to dial it back? Everyone is scared out of their minds."

Ray cleared his throat. "We all need to do what we can to keep it together until the transport arrives. We're relying on you to get things running well enough to keep everyone in this building safe until that happens."

Remo tightened his arms over his chest and stared at the floor.

"Good. What's possible then?"

"It's possible we're all going to fucking die out here."

"*Remo.*"

The room fell silent.

Ray leaned back in his chair and laced his hands over his stomach. "This isn't the way any of us wanted to start our day, trust me on that, but if you think it's bad now, it'll be a lot worse if Mr. Kennington gets here and we're all sitting on our hands."

Remo looked from Callen to Ray. "When is he in?"

Ray shrugged. "Not until tomorrow morning. Issues with the second pilot or something."

"And the first transport?"

"Should be on the way, or it will be shortly. A couple of hours out."

"So, when do we get out of here?"

"Once the non-essential staff are gone."

Remo shook his head and dropped his arms to his side. "For fuck's sake."

Callen took another step forward and stood next to Ray. "Listen, we want to get out of here as much as you do. So does everyone else stuck in the dark, waiting for you to get your ass in gear and do your fucking job." He pointed a rigid finger to his chest. "Unless you want to add me to your growing list of problems in life, take your little bag of tricks and get to it."

Ray held out a hand to Callen and spoke softly. "That's enough."

Callen took a step back, hands balled at his sides. His eyes focused on Remo, daring him to test his luck.

The shade of red on Remo's face darkened, but he held his tongue.

Ray collected his thoughts before speaking. "I'll ask again, what's possible?"

Remo shook his head and shrugged.

"The heat seems to still be working?"

"The passive system is."

"Okay." Ray looked to the ceiling. "What about the lights? Can anything be done about that?"

Remo wiped his sleeve under his nose. "Some of the lines were damaged, but I should be able to reroute at the control panel. Storage is non-existent compared to what we need. Should be able to get the basics back, but lights and ventilation might be the best case."

"Might?"

"Might is as good as you're gonna get until I dig into it."

Ray held both hands out flat. "Okay, okay." He glanced back to Callen. "What about the sub-basement?"

Callen frowned. "Not sure. Something I've been putting off."

Ray rubbed at his temple. "Shit." He sighed. "Okay, one thing at a time. Remo, please start on the panel. Let me know if there's anything we can help with."

Remo huffed and turned to look along the hall. "Yeah. Fine." Soon, his footsteps trailed away, and the room settled into silence.

"Cal?"

"Yeah?"

"Keep an eye on him."

Callen straightened the holster over his shoulders and followed Remo's path out the door.

EIGHT

Krystal stopped and set her bag on the snow by her feet. "Okay, Ellery and Darby," she pointed into a loose grouping of aspens, "see that tag?"

They looked up to a band of fluorescent nylon tied high on a bare branch and nodded.

"Right underneath is your blind." Kneeling, she unzipped her pack. From the top, she removed a black two-way radio with a digital screen and held it out. Ellery stepped forward, grabbed it by the antenna, then turned it back and forth in his hand.

Krystal zipped her pack and shouldered it. "Keep the volume down. Only use it if it's an emergency. You've got an alarm set for check-in?"

Darby gave her a thumbs up.

"Remember, only target out the front of the blind."

Darby nodded.

"Ellery?"

"Yeah, yeah. I got it."

Krystal turned and waded into the brush. "Let's go, Johnathan."

Johnathan looked to his friends, then adjusted the strap of his bag over his shoulder and followed behind her.

———

Johnathan sat with his hands stretched over a compact propane heater, his eyes trained out the window of the blind. "How long have we been here?"

Krystal untucked her arm and glanced at her watch. "Couple hours."

Johnathan's mouth twisted down on one side.

Krystal interlaced her fingers on her lap and straightened her back. "You know what you signed up for, right?"

"Oh, I do. Just thought things might happen…faster."

Krystal shrugged one shoulder. "Sorry, can't control the wildlife."

Johnathan smiled, lowering his gaze. "Really? I thought you were the best."

Krystal pursed her lips, but her eyes brightened. "Oh, I am."

Johnathan stole a quick glance to confirm her reaction. "How do you do it? Sit here for hours, doing nothing, saying nothing?"

"Practice."

"And you enjoy it?"

"The silence?" Krystal locked eyes with Johnathan. "I do."

Johnathan grinned and shook his head. When he focused back out on the trees, his expression flattened. Without breaking his gaze, he reached for his rifle and propped it on a shooting stick. Krystal knelt forward, balancing on one knee, and scanned for what held Johnathan's attention.

"Think I can take it down?"

Krystal caught sight of the antlers first, then through the maze of spindle tree trunks, a massive, deep brown form emerged. She whispered next to Johnathan's ear. "Don't you fucking dare."

Johnathan's neck straightened, and his face froze. "What? Why?"

"Not something you're owed an answer to, remember?" Krystal sat back against the nylon wall of the blind. "You're here for deer. Take that shot, and you'll start a war."

Jonathan swallowed hard.

Krystal peered beyond the wall in the direction of the second blind. "Hopefully, your buddies are smart enough to keep it in their pants."

Jonathan set the safety on his rifle, eased it down, and watched the moose disappear into the trees. "Hopefully."

Through the menagerie of framed glass, shadows swept along the ground in time with the slowing blades of the helicopter. Escaping heat from the engine rippled the air above it.

A line of people wound along the curved inside face of the building. Ray leaned against the reception desk with his arms crossed high while he shifted his attention between the front door and the line of anxious faces leading up to it.

From beneath the stairway to the upper level, Callen walked through a propped open service door. He backed up against the desk next to Ray with his hands tucked in the collar of his vest.

"Hey."

Ray nodded once. "Hey, Cal."

"What's the holdup?"

"Not sure. Helicopter stuff."

"Anyone come in?"

"No, the boss called off the security detail. Said we can handle it."

"Wonderful."

"Well, to be honest, they're not much more than figureheads."

"True."

Ray angled his head toward Callen. "Any word on the lights?"

"Not really. Remo says he's working on it, but when I checked on him, all he seemed to be doing was swearing a lot and throwing shit around."

"Everyone has their process."

"That they do."

A pilot in a heavy black jacket and dark tinted glasses walked up, rapped on the exterior door, then gave a thumbs-up.

Ray raised a hand in response and pushed away from the desk. "Finally."

Pulling his phone from his back pocket, he flipped to a recently typed note. "Looks like we're ready to go." He stood next to the door and held the phone in front of him. "Okay, let's see…"

His eyes matched names from the illuminated screen to the faces queued along the curved wall. At the last name, he paused and rescanned the line.

"Has anyone seen Isaac?"

Shrugs and shaking heads met Ray's question.

"Great. Okay, Leah, you can head on out. I'll go track him down."

At the head of the line, a woman picked up a small suitcase at her feet and stepped toward the front door. The others stood and stared until Ray waved them on. "Go, go, go."

Slipping his phone back into his pocket, he faced Callen. Ray opened his mouth to speak but paused when booming footsteps echoed down the service hall. A disheveled man ran into the lobby with a messenger bag hanging from a long strap over his shoulder.

Callen stepped away from the reception desk, his hands loose at his side, ready to move.

Struggling for air, the man bent forward with his hands on his knees. "Am I…too…late?"

Ray tilted his head. "Late for what?"

"The, uh, transport."

"Well, no, but the roster is already full."

The man stood upright and wiped beads of sweat from his forehead. "Yeah, about that. I, uh, kinda made a deal with my boy, Isaac. He'll catch the next one."

"Funny, he didn't say anything to me."

"Sorry, sort of a last-minute thing." The man's eyes shifted in every direction but Ray's.

"Okay, if you're sure." Ray took his phone out. "What was your name again?"

"Oh, Thorsten. Thorsten Wagner."

Ray's thumbs tapped against the screen. "Thorsten. Right…" His eyes turned up. "You always wear shorts?"

A laugh crackled in Thorsten's throat. "Yeah, sort of my thing."

The front door eased shut as the last of those in line filed outside to the waiting helicopter.

Ray lowered his phone and motioned toward the exit. "Better hurry then."

"Right. Thanks." Thorsten winced, holding an arm across his stomach as he stepped away.

Ray watched him closely. "You okay?"

Thorsten rushed for the exit. "Yeah, just a, uh, just a cramp. The running and all." He darted through the door and into the light.

TEN

Shadows changed their angles to the east. Johnathan's eyes threatened to shut when the crack of a breaking branch brought him to attention. Holding her finger to her lips, Krystal pointed out the front of the blind.

An eight-point whitetail took careful steps through the trees less than thirty meters from the blind. Its wide, brown eyes scanned the undergrowth as it took cautious steps. Moving in slow motion, Johnathan positioned his rifle on the shooting stick and rested his finger on the trigger as he sighted. Krystal crouched to one side behind him.

Hesitating at first, she leaned close to whisper in Johnathan's ear. "Don't forget to breathe." Krystal pushed back without a sound.

Johnathan's finger twitched. The buck's ears perked, and in a flash, it launched forward and disappeared deep into the trees.

"Damn." Johnathan let out a long, slow breath and raised up from the scope on his rifle.

Krystal bent through the window of the blind and scanned the sky.

"What is it?"

She wiped at her nose. "Quiet."

"Helicopter?"

Krystal cast a hard gaze into the distance. "Yeah."

"Seems…close, right?"

"Too close. Stay down."

Soon, hammering metal blades pulsed a deafening beat. A black mass eclipsed the sun as it broke across the sky from the north and banked overhead. Krystal caught a glimpse of the pilot through the blood-stained windshield. The tail spun to the sky, then seemed to freeze for a split second. Shredding wood and metal shrouded the treeline as the helicopter fell. Upon impact, a fireball bloomed into the sky.

Krystal rose on her knees and shuffled toward the exit.

Johnathan held out a hand. "What are you doing?"

"I need to go check it out."

"But—"

Krystal scowled. "Stay here."

Johnathan frowned and lowered his arm.

Krystal burst through the door of the blind and ran in the direction of the billowing, dark cloud. When the flicker of the burning wreckage was visible through the trees, Krystal readied her rifle. As she eased toward the crash site, heat from the flames brushed her face. She circled in a wide perimeter. It looked to be private, expensive looking, not military. Parts of the tail protruded from the higher branches. It showed American markings, but something looked off about them.

Blood washed over the pilot's clothing and the charred skin on his face. His helmet bubbled and melted as fire overtook the rest of the cabin. Bodies twisted in a pile at the bottom of the fuselage. Two others, maybe three, spread around the crash site. Walking the area, Krystal scanned high in the trees one last time. A branch broke behind her. Spinning down to one knee, she sighted her rifle.

Ellery froze with his hands up, and Darby skittered behind him.

Krystal aimed the rifle away from the men. "What the hell are you doing here?"

"Holy shit, just like in the movies." Ellery's mouth and eyes were wide.

Darby peered around Ellery's shoulder and focused on the shattered windscreen of the helicopter. "Is he…are they dead?"

Krystal stood and slipped the strap of the rifle over her shoulder. "Where the hell is—" She turned and flinched back. "*Jesus fucking Christ.*"

Johnathan held his hands out in front of him. "Sorry, I—"

Krystal snarled and pointed a finger. "What did I say when we got here? You get home safe and sound with a trophy to prove to your stupid friends how manly you are *if* you do what I tell you."

She broke her gaze and pushed aside the emotions welling up inside her. Scanning the northern sky, she caught sight of another column of smoke. Faint and lazy, but still active.

"I'm really sorry. We just wanted to see if we could help."

Krystal pulled up on the cuffs of her gloves. "We need to get back to camp. *Now.*"

Johnathan and Ellery looked from each other to the burning machine, then followed behind Krystal. Darby stared off into the trees and raised one hand to bite his fingernails.

Krystal paused and turned. "Darby?"

He did not respond. Even in the glow of the wreckage, he looked pale.

"Darby, look at me."

Darby raised his eyes to Krystal.

"You all right there?"

He pointed a well-chewed finger into the trees. "There's someone over that way."

"Yeah, I know—"

"No. I think they're moving."

Krystal sighed and dropped her shoulders. She proceeded toward the spot Darby had motioned to, stepping high over brush and dead branches. A body rested in a pocket between large, twisted trunks. Krystal held one arm across her face to help block the smell of burning hair and flesh. Heavy canvas shorts had soaked with blood but were otherwise undamaged. Cuts and burns littered the exposed skin on the man's arms and legs. Patches of skin showing on his back bled halos of yellow and crimson. Dark hair matted with gore seeping from various wounds on his scalp. Each shallow breath held congestion and struggle, until the last breath caught, his body twitched, and he fell still.

Krystal left the cover of the trees and headed back to the group. Her customers stared as she stormed past them in the direction of the blind. When they did not move, she stopped. "What the fuck are you people waiting for?"

"Shouldn't we do something?"

"Do something? What skills do you bring to this situation exactly? Can you use the power of your mind to bring actual help? How about bringing back the dead?"

With no adequate reply to offer, they fell silent, making no attempt to look at each other or Krystal.

Krystal pinched the bridge of her nose. "Listen, I don't

have time to babysit. We need to get back to camp." She craned her neck forward to lock eyes with each of them. "*Now.*"

The group nodded in unison.

"Until we get back to the truck, we probably won't get a signal to call anyone, let alone someone who can do something about this." She checked the angle of the sun and clouds building to the west. "We lock down until morning, then get the hell out as soon as the sun comes up. I've got a decent enough idea of the coordinates. We can call it in when we get back to town."

The men shuffled their feet behind Krystal as she disappeared into the trees.

The group ate a simple dinner in silence. Krystal paid little attention to the others. Her mind raced, searching for a reasonable explanation while at the same time working out a plan for what might come next. As Ellery and Johnathan continued to pick at their plates, she swiped her own clean with a scrap of bread, then set it on the ground.

Darby sat with his plate on his lap, untouched, and stared off into the night. One knee bounced like a Geiger counter in a nuclear minefield. The constant vibration shifted the plate close to falling. As he came to his senses, his hand shot out to brace the edge. Darby's eyes darted to the others before settling on the bare dirt in front of him. He cleared his throat, but his voice still cracked as he spoke. "I need to use the washroom." He stood and set the plate on his seat. Pulling down the bottom of his jacket, Darby wandered away from the camp.

Ellery leaned toward Johnathan. "You think he's okay?"

One side of Johnathan's mouth turned down. "Should he be?"

"Well, no, but…"

"That's probably all that needs to be said then."

Ellery held his lips tight and shrugged.

Krystal looked up to the two men as if she had forgotten they were there. Checking her watch, she sighed. "We should all turn in. Get packed up and be ready to head out at sunrise."

"Okay." Johnathan looked out into the surrounding night. "What about Darby?"

"What about him?"

"Should we wait for him?"

"Maybe he needs a break from you two. Ever think about that?"

Johnathan scratched the side of his head. "Okay. See you in the morning."

Ellery stood with his plate in his hand.

"Leave it. I'll take care of it."

"You sure?"

Krystal smiled with her mouth, but not with her eyes. "Good night, Ellery."

Ellery shrugged, grinning. "Sure, okay." He rested the plate on the stump he had used as a seat. "Thanks. Have a good night."

Krystal watched as the two men went behind the cabin door and the small window glowed with faint light. She sat forward and released a heavy sigh.

Growing clouds obscured the moon and stars. The air held a tinge that gave the impression it might snow. Few sounds were heard over the crackle of the dying fire until Darby returned.

He stumbled out of the thicker brush, watching the ground. Holding that focus through vacant eyes, he tracked across the open area of the campsite. Darby pushed into the cabin, and the door slammed shut behind him.

Krystal watched the cabin, waiting for more. After the light inside faded, she stood to collect dirty plates, then tossed them in the fire. When the flames finally died down, Krystal stirred the remaining coals with a stick and poured a pot of water over the top. After packing up the leftovers, she walked off into the trees.

ELEVEN

Krystal jerked awake. She reached out and pulled the stock of her rifle close.

"Krystal?"

She scanned through the thin wall of the tent. The darkness outside allowed no shadows or signs of movement.

"Krystal? Are you here?"

Krystal let out a slow breath. "Yeah. Be out in a minute." She unzipped her sleeping bag and flipped it open. After checking her watch, she drew her knees in and put on a fresh pair of wool socks. Impatient pacing in the snow offered a soundtrack while she laced up her boots.

With the flap of the tent held aside, she paused to look through the trees. Johnathan stood alone, five or six meters out. Krystal snaked her way out of her hiding spot and halted a few paces away from him. "What's up?"

"Hey. Um, well, it's Darby."

Krystal raised an eyebrow. "What about him?"

"He's gone."

"What do you mean, gone?"

"I mean, he took off. Packed up his stuff and left."

"How could he…" Krystal's voice trailed off as she retraced her steps from the night before. Something had felt off, but she was too tired and distracted to listen to the little voice in her head. "Give me a second."

She dashed back to her tent, knelt in the opening, then tossed blankets and overturned bags. When she stopped, her heart hammered in her ears. "Shit."

She stormed back toward Johnathan with her rifle over her shoulder. "Let's go."

Johnathan stammered but soon gave up on the attempt to speak and followed along.

At the campsite, Krystal burst through the door of the small cabin. Ellery bolted upright and drew in a sharp breath. "What? What's going on?"

Krystal pulled the sheets from the far bed. She bent to look below the thin frame and mattress. Patting the surface under it, she palmed an empty pill bottle and stood. The label was dirty and worn, like it had been reused a few too many times.

"When did he leave?"

"I don't know, before five, I guess. Maybe a little over an hour ago."

Ellery rubbed at his eye. "He woke me up a couple of times talking to himself."

"Yeah, not sure if he slept at all."

Krystal stared at the floor and let out a sharp exhale. "Not helpful."

Johnathan shrugged. "Sorry."

Krystal waved him away. "It's not you. It's your dipshit friend."

"Well, he's not really—"

"Don't care." Krystal stepped away from the empty cot and paused in the open door frame. "I need to go check on the truck. You two, stay here."

Johnathan nodded. "Sure."

Krystal locked eyes with Ellery and pointed a rigid finger at the wooden floorboards. "Right here."

Ellery scratched at his temple. "Can we at least go out to pee?"

Krystal turned and rolled her eyes. Without responding, she walked outside and was greeted by the first signs of the morning sun as it breached the horizon.

———

Krystal fought to catch her breath as she cleared the trees. She ran the whole length of the river, even though she knew what to expect. Fresh tire tracks snaked out of the small clearing. Broken branches and displaced snow marked where the truck pushed too far off the path, but it was gone all the same. Krystal traced along the ruts until she arrived at the road. The tracks continued south, and no sign of the truck could be seen or heard.

Krystal dug her cold fingertips into the palms of her gloves. Her teeth clenched until the strain on her jaw radiated across her vision.

Tugging off her glove and tucking it under her arm, she pulled up on her pocket zipper and took out her cell phone. The screen lit up, but the top left-hand corner showed no service.

"Shit."

Krystal wandered down the middle of the road, waving the phone high over her head. She saw a single bar flicker in and out, so she swiped to make a call. With it pressed to her ear, she turned to glance both ways along the road. The tone broke and crackled, but after the seventh ring, it connected.

"Hey, it's Clint. Leave a message, and I'll call you back."

Krystal let out a slow breath as she waited to speak. "Clint, it's Krystal. Listen, we've got a problem—"

Three beeps sounded, and the call disconnected. Krystal held the phone in front of her. The no service icon had returned.

"*Damnit.*"

Without another word, she followed her own tracks back the way she had come.

———

Johnathan stepped out of the cabin as Krystal stalked past. She was at the cookhouse before he spoke up.

"I was starting to get worried."

Krystal's pace slowed, and she stopped. She considered if he was worried for her, or because they would be stranded alone in the middle of the northern Ontario wilderness with not enough sense to survive.

"What did you find?"

Krystal tucked her chin to her chest and looked to Johnathan from the corner of her eye. "Nothing."

Ellery stuck his head out from the cabin doorway. "He's gone?"

"He's gone. So is the truck."

Ellery's ever-present smile faltered. "Oh shit."

Johnathan crossed his arms. "What do we do now?"

"I need to eat. Then I guess I'll have to figure something out."

———

Krystal pushed the remaining pile of canned stew around on her plate. Johnathan and Ellery had long since finished their own and sat watching wisps of smoke curl and twist before fading away. Ellery attempted conversation more than once, but soon enough figured out the benefits of being quiet.

Krystal set her fork on her plate, then reached down to leave both on the ground. She brushed her hands together and licked her teeth. "Okay. Let's talk about what we're going to do."

Ellery straightened, and Johnathan nodded, leaning forward on his elbows. They waited for instructions, but Krystal froze in place.

Ellery looked sidelong at Johnathan, then back to Krystal. "What—"

Krystal raised a hand to silence him, then slowly turned her eyes to the sky. The pounding of helicopter blades grew until both Ellery and Johnathan covered their ears. Krystal watched the black machine crest the creaking branches high in the trees and arc away to the north. Just out of sight, the rhythm changed. Soon, it circled back, the belly flashing into view before it resumed its path and flew away.

Krystal looked down at the two men focusing on her with wide eyes. She snuck a brief glance at the sun and its position above them. "Change of plans."

"What plan?"

Krystal frowned at Ellery. "I've been trying to figure out a way to get you out of here. We've run out of time for today."

Johnathan checked his watch, then shielded his eyes as he looked to the sky. "You don't think we'd make it?"

"No offense, but to get packed up and out to where the

truck was parked, we're looking at an hour and a half, maybe two. Fully geared up, there's no way we'll get close enough to civilization or have time for anyone to come get us before the sun goes down."

"Can't we call someone?"

"I tried. Not sure if it went through, and I can't risk it without knowing."

"So, what do we do?"

"*I'm* going for a little hike to find out where that chopper is heading." She moved her pointer finger between them. "You two are going to rest up and get ready to leave."

"But—"

"Stop." Krystal groaned and rubbed at her temple. "You're going to follow anyway, aren't you?"

Ellery and Johnathan looked at each other and shrugged.

Krystal put her hands on her hips and turned away. "Fine. Get some food and water to bring along, I'll be back in a minute. I need to grab some things."

TWELVE

Ray looked up to the man standing in his office doorway. His fur hunter's cap, with the front buttoned up and the side flaps down, came close to touching the top. The sleeves of his plain t-shirt stretched tight over toned biceps as he raised his arms and pressed against the top of the frame. A polished chrome belt buckle caught the light as he moved, and from behind an unzipped puffy gray vest, a holstered gun stuck out.

Ray returned his attention to his paperwork. "Good to see you, Linford."

"Is it? I certainly didn't want to see your sorry ass again so soon."

Ray shrugged. "Yeah, well, I wish it was under better circumstances. Come on in."

Linford lowered his arms and strode into the room. He kicked a chair away from the wall and slumped down.

"Where's the boss?"

"Doing damage control. He needed to talk to the pilot, not sure why. Things are a little tense."

"I can imagine."

"So, they really didn't radio in for help?"

Ray straightened the papers in front of him and set them in a tiered tray to his left. "No. Nothing. Then again, communication is a little…inconsistent at the moment."

Linford looked away. "Right. Nothin' seems to be going your way right now."

"You don't know the half of it."

"Why? What else?"

"Staff are getting weird about the situation. Things are going missing, and we found someone tied up in their room. The guy he was bunking with took his spot on the last ride out."

"That didn't really work out for him, did it?"

"No." Ray sighed and ran a hand over his hair. "Plus, one of the pens got busted open."

"Serious? Shit." Linford adjusted his position in the chair. "The chopper's secure. Besides, the sun's out, right?"

Ray's head bobbed a nearly imperceptible nod.

"Hey, what do you know that I don't?"

"Nothing. I mean…I don't know. I heard they've been messing with the formula. Some of the staff have seen things that don't add up."

"Like?"

Ray frowned and scratched at his forearm. "I don't know. It could all be gossip, you know?"

"And what if it's not?"

"Then I guess we need to be more careful."

"Fuck me." Linford drew in a breath and sat up straight. "Well, I'm going to go find your shadow before we get this show on the road."

"He should be on the staff level keeping an eye on the repairs."

Linford looked to Ray from the corner of his eyes. "What about the sub-basement?"

"Everything is under control. So far."

"So far." Linford shook his head as he stood. "You motherfuckers. I don't even know."

"Hey, Linford?"

Linford stopped just past the threshold. "Yeah."

"Be careful."

"Yeah, Ray. You too."

THIRTEEN

Inside the cabin, Ellery fussed with the woodstove for something to do. Johnathan sat next to the front door with a clear line of sight to the camp through the small window. His breath became shallow, and his head lolled once before motion outside grabbed his attention.

At first, he did not recognize the person striding toward him. A mottled green hood draped over their head, and heavy goggles covered their eyes. Every belt and buckle on their jacket and pants were cinched tight, and leather guards covered their forearms and neck. A rifle hung tight to the low-profile pack across their back. It was not until Johnathan caught a wisp of sandy-brown hair sticking out that he realized it was Krystal. He leaned forward, close to the glass.

Ellery looked up from the book in his hands. "What's up?"

"Nothing. Krystal's back."

"And?"

"I don't know. She looks…over-prepared."

"Umm, okay?"

Krystal halted outside of the cabin entrance.

"Guess that's our cue." Ellery jumped up, zipping his coat to his chin.

"Yeah." Johnathan pushed himself up and opened the door. Nodding, he put his hands in his pockets.

"You guys ready?"

"Think so. Should we bring our guns?"

"No, I don't think that's a good idea."

"Okay."

Johnathan stepped into the cold. Ellery shut the cabin door behind him and followed along.

———

Krystal swung her rifle forward when she spotted debris from the crash. Her pace slowed, and she scanned for any small detail out of place. Moments later, the carcass of the helicopter came into view. A light dusting of snow covered it, and delicate icicles stretched down from the metalwork. The cockpit had frozen into a macabre tangle of warped metal and charred bodies.

She circled her own tracks around the wreckage. At the spot in the brush that Darby had pointed out, she stopped. Packed snow, stained red, trailed off deeper into the trees. Krystal faced Ellery and Johnathan, waiting a few paces away.

"Stay here a minute. I'll be right back."

Not waiting for a response, she stepped high, wading into the bushes. A pungent smell washed over her before she found the end of the tracks. Krystal reached inside the leather collar around her neck, pulled a bandanna over her nose, and advanced.

The man laid face down with no sign of breath or

movement. What remained of his skin was pallid. One arm reached out, the urge to continue strong until the end. Krystal did a quick search of the trees around him, then rejoined the others.

Johnathan pushed up on the brim of his hat. "Did you find anything?"

Krystal shrugged as she pulled the bandanna down, but avoided eye contact. "Nothing new. Doesn't look like it's been touched since yesterday."

"If that other chopper was checking on them, wouldn't they have sent help?"

Krystal let various scenarios run through her mind. "If they were able to, you'd think so."

Johnathan swallowed and stared at the ground.

Ellery sighed. "So, what now?"

Krystal looked at the treeline to the north. "I still want to see where they were headed."

"Is that a good idea?"

"Once I have a better idea of what's going on, then we can head back."

Ellery frowned. "Okay."

"You don't have to come if you don't want to."

"You sure about that?"

The comment Krystal wanted to make circled her brain before she pushed it away. "You had a choice. Still do."

"No, you're right. It's fine." Ellery set his hands on his hips, and a hint of a smile surfaced. "We'll be back before dinner, right?"

Krystal turned away from him. "I'll do what I can."

"Sweet." Ellery checked the space behind him. "Before we go, I need to use the little boy's room."

Krystal raised an eyebrow. "Good thing you've got a lot of options then."

Ellery's smile widened into a toothy grin. "Be right back."

He sauntered toward the aft end of the helicopter wreckage, shaking the sleeves of his jacket down over his hands.

"No." Krystal motioned in the opposite direction. "Go that way."

Ellery's pace slowed, but he did not stop. Instead, he looped around. "Okay."

Krystal counted fourteen steps into the trees before Ellery hiked up his jacket and unzipped. Even as deep as he was, she caught his relieved head tilt, and steam wafting in the light breeze as the stream cut through untouched snow. The relief lasted only a moment, though.

Branches of a nearby bush rustled. Ellery's whole body flinched. A streak of white and gray shot out and disappeared into the dense trees.

"Holy shit."

He zipped his fly with shaking hands before stumbling away. With one eye focused behind him, he fixed the rest of his clothing and scurried to join the others. He returned flushed and out of breath.

Johnathan held out his hand. "Hey, you okay?"

Ellery pressed a closed fist over his pounding heart. "I...I don't know. Saw a bird or something. Maybe a squirrel. Scared the shit out of me."

"Oh." Johnathan relaxed. "Well, I guess you'd probably want to get the hell out of the way if someone tried to piss on you too."

Ellery's eyes widened, and he pushed out a slow breath. "Yeah, I guess."

"Are you two about done?"

Johnathan and Ellery looked to Krystal. Her feet spread wide, and she gripped her rifle with both hands. They each nodded, then averted their eyes.

The snap and thrum of helicopter blades grew from the north.

"*Get down.*"

They each tucked themselves beside the closest tree. Soon after, another black belly appeared in the sky. The blades pushed hard as it gained altitude and sped off in the general direction of civilization.

As the noise subsided, Johnathan shielded his eyes and scanned the sky. "What the hell is going on?"

Krystal retraced the helicopter's path. "Not sure. I haven't seen air traffic like this before."

"It's got to be military, right?"

"Don't think so. Not ours anyway."

"Weird."

"Yeah, a little."

Ellery pulled his toque back on his head. "So, what now?"

Krystal craned her neck toward the column of smoke fading to the north.

"You think someone will be there that can help us out?"

"Don't know. As far as I'm aware, there's not supposed to be any infrastructure this far out. Maybe they don't want to be found."

"Oh."

"Listen," Krystal propped her rifle against a tree and slipped her pack off, "let's get something to eat and rest up for a few minutes."

"Then what?"

"Then we go find out what's on fire."

The sun, muted by opaque, gray clouds, dipped to the top of the treeline as Krystal caught her first glimpse of the building. She crouched low, motioned for Johnathan and Ellery to do the same, then crept behind an old tree with a wide trunk.

The building was a giant black slab dropped into the middle of the wilderness, a collection of sharp right angles, except for the nearest end that was capped in a geodesic dome. Modern and sleek, it could not have been more out of place. Straight treelines ran twenty meters out from each side. A stretch of tall fence with razor wire coiled along the top was tucked at the back. Smoke trailed from the rear corner, but the bulk of the structure hid the source.

Johnathan removed a water bottle from his pack and drained it.

Next to him, Ellery sat and stretched out his legs while he leaned back on his gloved hands. "What do you figure?"

Johnathan raised an eyebrow. "What do you mean?"

"You want to ask her, or should I?"

"Uh…" Johnathan stole a glance at Krystal's back.

"I meant if we should go back to camp. What did you think I was saying?"

"Oh. Nothing."

Krystal lowered a pair of compact binoculars from her eyes. "I can hear you."

Johnathan blushed, though it showed little through the color already built in his cheeks from the cold.

Ellery sat forward and brushed the snow from his gloves. "So, can we go?"

Krystal slid the binoculars into a pocket on her pack. "Not yet. I want to take a closer look."

Johnathan studied the skyline to either side. "Won't it be dark soon?"

"Soon enough. I only need a few minutes. Either it's good, and we find help, or it's not, and we get back to camp."

"You sure?"

Krystal stared at Ellery.

He put his hands up with his palms flat. "Okay, you're the boss."

"Do I need to remind the two of you that you wanted to come along?"

"Well…"

"Good, that's settled then." Standing, Krystal shouldered her rifle. "Up. Let's go."

By the time Ellery finished grumbling to himself and was ready to move out, Johnathan had already followed Krystal with his thumbs tucked under the straps of his pack.

"Don't worry about me. I'll catch up, I guess." When neither Johnathan nor Krystal turned to acknowledge him, Ellery sighed and took long strides along their tracks in the snow to bridge the distance.

FOURTEEN

Twenty minutes into the flight, the nervous energy of the passengers had released, and the chatter died down. They turned to their books, music, or the inside of their eyelids—all except one.

Behind the pilot, a stocky man remained focused out the windshield. Fat fingers, filled with gold rings, tugged at one ear. He leaned forward with his elbows on his knees.

"Flying a little low, ain't you?"

The pilot glanced back but did not answer.

"Flightpath seems off too." The man ran a hand over slicked-back silver hair. "It's just, I've been on this run enough to notice." He stuck a thumb over his shoulder. "Not that any of these nutsacks would know. Zombies can't keep their faces out of their goddamned electronics."

The tempo of the blades changed as the craft banked slightly to the right, and toward a lake with a hundred crooked fingers of water wandering away from it.

"Where's Monty, anyway? I expected he'd be on this run."

The pilot flipped switches on the control panel in front of

him and overhead. Multiple lights went dark while others flickered to life. The man drew further forward in his seat as the helicopter slowed. Flicking a final switch, the pilot unbuckled and turned to the passenger compartment as he stood.

The man pushed back in his seat. "What the hell are you doing…" He stammered as his eyes darted between the pilot and the buckle of his seatbelt while he fumbled with it.

The pilot retrieved a handgun with a short, rectangular slide from the holster on his leg. Raising the gun, he squeezed the trigger. The stocky man went limp as the bullet caved his forehead in. The pilot fired again and again in precise movements. In the back row, a tall, thin man managed to unlatch his seatbelt and scramble to the aisle before he collapsed. The others held fast in their seats, eyes vacant, faces slack and flecked with blood, their own or their neighbor's.

As the air cleared, the pilot ejected the clip, tucked it away in a pocket, and replaced it with another. Holstering the gun, he stepped to the side door.

When the door slid open, frigid wind swirled through the passenger compartment. The pilot started with the woman slumped in the nearest seat. He undid her seatbelt, grabbed her shoulders, and pulled her body forward and past him. Her arms and legs spun away, her body breaking through the thin layer of ice over the lake like a starfish. Before the surface had time to settle, the next body hit and sank. Five more followed in short order. The last passenger was the stocky man with silver hair. The pilot pulled him onto the floor by one ankle, jerked the man forward until his legs dangled over the edge of the door. The pilot repositioned, grasping the backs of the seats behind him. With the heel of his boot planted on the man's shoulder, he kicked. The man's falling body impacted the water before he made a full rotation in the air.

The door slammed shut, and the pilot sat back behind the controls. He tightened the straps on his harness and reversed the positions of most of the switches that he had recently adjusted. With one hand on the pitch control, he pulled a satellite phone from his vest and dialed. His back straightened when the call connected.

"Yes, sir."

A pause.

"Yes, sir. It's done."

Another pause.

"Tomorrow morning, as planned."

With a click, the line fell dead, so the pilot tucked the phone away. He made one last check of the machine's instruments and flipped the last of the switches. The engine whined as the helicopter turned south and pushed high into the sky.

FIFTEEN

Krystal guided Johnathan and Ellery along the building's left side, moving slow as she scanned their surroundings. Security cameras, tucked behind blackened glossy domes, were spaced along the length of the building. No lights or movement could be seen behind the large, tinted glass panels lining the upper level. Halfway along, a door with no exterior handle broke the smooth panel of the wall. They saw another similar door near the far corner. The main level had no other openings. No tracks showed in the snow ahead of them.

Ellery slid the tips of his gloved hand along the smooth surface of the exterior wall. He stopped to pull one glove off and set his hand flat against it. Krystal paused to look back.

"It's warm."

Krystal pushed her hood back. "And?"

Ellery leaned close to examine the wall. "I think it's some type of solar collector."

Johnathan scratched at the top of his head. "A solar panel?"

"Not like one I've seen before, but I think so." Ellery smiled. "That's really cool."

They continued on to the far corner in silence. Ellery and Johnathan stayed back as Krystal made her way into the open space and the haze of bitter smoke. She stood in front of a chain-link wall, twice her height. From a distance, she had not noticed another fence two meters inside the perimeter, topped with coiled razor wire, or the second enclosure built next to it. A third of the way down the fence line, a tower with a covered platform perched between the enclosures, just above the top of the fence. Steep metal steps trailed from the platform to the ground. Snow covered signs warned of danger, and stylized lightning bolts confirmed the electric nature of the inside fence, though the indicator lights posted at each corner were unlit.

"Is…is that an axe?"

Krystal followed the direction of Johnathan's pointed finger. As swirling snow cleared with the shifting breeze, it came into view. Hung from a low branch of a leafless tree, knotted jute rope gripped the end of a handle, and its rusted head swayed below. Krystal spotted other objects further back in the enclosure, but it was hard to make out definitive shapes through branches and smoke. One could have been a baseball bat. Another, a mace.

"What the hell is that for?"

"Not sure."

Krystal examined the inside corner of the enclosure. A slanted entrance pointed into the ground like a cellar at an old farmhouse. The section beside it had one as well, and both faced the open area between the enclosures and the main building. Walking on, she focused her attention around her feet, as if the earth would open and offer up its secrets. She stopped where the enclosures met and turned to the building. The wall looked much like the rest, except for the recessed upper level capped with two flat glass panels.

"Krystal?"

"What?" Krystal's voice came quieter than she meant.

She spotted Ellery and Johnathan standing at the corner of the building and motioned them over. "Yeah, come on." She pulled her bandanna up and adjusted her goggles over her eyes.

Not checking to see if they followed, she walked on. The next corner of the building was eclipsed by a massive cage constructed with thick steel pipe and perforated metal sheets. Dark smoke flowed from beneath the charred and warped enclosure. On either side of it, the walls of the building buckled and split. Wires and fibers glowed and sparked underneath. Krystal watched as the infection of fire crept outward from the source like a web of molten lava.

Ticks and pings echoed out from the smoldering machinery as she swept a wide circle around it. With her gun at the ready, she stretched her neck to see around the corner. The other side appeared to be a carbon copy, save for the cleared off helipad at the far end. Away from the side of the building at the tree's edge, a smaller structure with a row of roll-up doors showed damage. Part of it had collapsed in on itself, and wisps of smoke drifted around the places still standing.

Dull hammering from the main building forced her attention. She held out her hand for Ellery and Johnathan to stay put, then shouldered her gun and took a few slow steps forward. The thumping stopped, and so did Krystal. Strained breathing filled the quiet air. Krystal adjusted her footing, crunching the snow as it compacted under her boots.

"H…hello?"

Krystal held her breath.

"Please. I…I'm just trying to get out. The door is blocked."

Krystal scanned the length of the building. "What's going on here?"

A sound of relief came from behind the door. "Mechanical failure. The power is out. Please, I just need to get the door open."

Krystal paused, then completed her arc until the door came into view. A panel from the mechanical area had bent down and prevented the door from moving more than a crack. Only an eye showed in the sliver of darkness.

"What is this place?"

The man behind the door cleared his throat. "It's a, uh, retreat. A hotel."

"In the middle of nowhere?"

A pause.

"Who are you? Where did you come from?"

Krystal debated how much to share. "Hunting party. We're lost. Just trying to get home."

The man pressed closer to the door. "I can help you. The helicopter will be back soon. Please, I need to get out of here."

Krystal lowered her rifle, but not all the way, and stepped back. She fixed her gaze on the eye behind the door but angled her face away. "Johnathan. Ellery."

Bounding around the corner at her call, the two came to stand by her side.

"What's up?"

She motioned at the door. "There's someone stuck inside." She hesitated. "We need to get them out."

Ellery's eyes widened. "What? Really?" He moved closer to the door. "Holy shit, yeah." He waved Johnathan over. "Come on, man. Let's do this."

Johnathan glanced to Krystal, then walked beside Ellery, testing the weight of the metal panel. "You ready?"

"Yeah, let's go."

"Okay. One, two…"

They put their weight into the panel, pushing it up and out of the way. Straining, they fought to keep their footing as the metal groaned. When it had reached the end of its travel, Johnathan stumbled back, gulping for air. "Is that good?"

The top corner of the door clanged against the bent metal. Ellery pulled the toque from his head and wiped away perspiration. "One more go?"

"We can try. Not sure how much more it will give."

Johnathan positioned himself to one side and reached high. Ellery rocked back, then threw himself into the obstruction. A roar built in his throat as he bore down with his shoulder low. His legs began to shake, but just as they were about to give, the assembly jumped, and the door snapped open.

The man pushed past Ellery and Johnathan and ran into the gray light. Krystal skirted around to the other side of the door. The man stopped out in the fresh snow and faced the trio with his feet and hands held wide. Bloodshot eyes darted between each of them, and slowly, a grin came to his face. Something caught his attention in the direction of the chain-link enclosure, and the smile faded. He stammered, then fumbled a handgun from his pocket. Raising it with an unsteady hand, he squeezed the trigger.

Ellery retreated into the open doorway. "What the…"

Krystal moved next to Johnathan and grabbed his shoulder

as another shot rang out. She pushed him into Ellery. "Inside. Now."

Pulling the door shut behind her, she backed away from it. Gunshots were replaced with shouting, a cry for help, both dulled through the thick door.

"Shit."

Krystal pulled her goggles off and dropped them to the floor, then searched the pockets and pouches of her pack. Her fingers found a small aluminum cylinder, and she pressed down on one end. The space glowed with focused but harsh white light. Pointing the flashlight at the ground, the edges of the beam highlighted drawn faces and wide eyes.

"Krystal, what—"

"Shut up."

"But—"

"*I said shut your mouth.*"

Standing rigid, Ellery nodded.

Krystal turned to the door. She ran her free hand down the length of the frame, finding no handle or visible latch. The only deviation from the otherwise smooth surface laid just below eye level. Near the edge, a plastic circle sat flush in the wall, glossy with a smaller matte circle in the middle.

Johnathan cleared his throat. "Doesn't look like we're getting out here."

Krystal pulled her hand away and sighed. "No."

Turning, she raised the flashlight to her right. Inside a propped open door, a narrow staircase led both up and down from where they stood. The elevator on the other side of it showed a broken door hanging at a slight angle. A wisp of smoke drifted from the gap. Three service carts stacked with folded linens were lined up beside it. Further back, a hall curved and disappeared around the corner.

Krystal refocused the light to her left. A long hall opened before her, though the length hid past the short range of the flashlight. A doorless passageway near them led into an open space. Another was positioned a short distance along the corridor. She pressed the face of the flashlight against her side, then sidled up to the first passage. The darkness gave the sensation of space, but nothing more. She leaned in for a better look.

Ellery whispered behind her. "Anything?"

Krystal gave a brief glance to the men huddled behind her. "Yeah, I don't know."

"What do we do?"

"Don't have much of a choice."

Johnathan's voice cracked. "I mean, what are we walking into? Why was that guy trying to get out like that?"

"I know as much as you do, but I guess we're about to find out."

Krystal brought her rifle forward and held the light against the forestock, following the barrel's aim. She eased around the corner and swept the room. Large textured tiles in the hall transitioned to intricate plush carpet. The ceiling stretched away, with clusters of colorful glass shades hanging from long metal fixtures.

A giant glass dome took up the near end of the sizable room. Water spots speckled the inside of the glass. The narrow beam from Krystal's flashlight reflected through it, creating strange shadows, but it was otherwise empty. Sets of luxurious curved benches surrounded the perimeter. The video cameras lining the top, pointed inward.

Similar openings to the one they had walked through were positioned strategically along the opposite wall. Massive TV screens filled the space between each one.

With the beam of the flashlight focused down the length of the building, Krystal continued on. Johnathan shuffled behind her, and Ellery hopped to keep up.

"Are those poker tables?"

"Looks that way."

Johnathan whispered. "Well, the guy said it was some kind of resort, right?"

"He said retreat."

"Same thing. Sorta?"

"Not really."

Krystal walked past huge potted tropical plants. They offered some amount of separation to a grouping of round tables, each with four perfectly placed high-back chairs around. Beyond them, a fully stocked bar and an open kitchen with racks of copper pots suspended over shiny stainless counters.

"This is pretty nice."

"Maybe with the lights on. At the moment, creepy is the word I would use."

As they neared the end of the room, Krystal slowed. To the left, around a bump-out in the wall, a closed set of double doors blocked the way. An opening in the long wall next to them led to another staircase. Krystal turned to confirm their options. "Come on."

Neither Ellery nor Johnathan said a word while following like ducklings keeping up with their mother. At the nearest opening on the right-hand wall, she peered both ways to find another corridor with the familiar textured tile floor and plain walls. For the first time, she noticed discreet sensors on the inside of the entry. They reminded her of anti-theft devices used at the mall.

"Shit." Krystal sighed. "Which way?"

Johnathan shrugged. "I don't know."

Ellery sidled up between them, barely able to contain his smile. "Dealer's choice?"

Johnathan groaned.

Krystal muttered under her breath and took a left through the opening. Aiming her rifle low, she moved with cautious steps, and led them along the corridor toward the front of the building. They continued past a narrow hallway that dead-ended with a trio of closed doors, only to stop a short distance later.

Krystal held her hand against yet another locked door. "Let's head straight back on this side."

Krystal passed between Ellery and Johnathan. The flashlight hung from her wrist with the halo of the light bouncing from wall to wall. It caught a reflection further along their path, and she froze.

Johnathan stopped behind her and set a hand on her shoulder. He leaned in close and whispered. "What's wrong?"

Krystal tightened her grip on the rifle and leveled the barrel. She did not respond.

Ahead of them, a stoic voice reached out from the dark. "I think I'm what's wrong."

Johnathan recoiled.

"Gun down. Now."

Krystal sneered. "You first."

The formless voice chuffed. "Not a chance."

"What is this place?"

"How did you get in here?"

"We walked."

"Out for a Sunday stroll?"

"Something like that."

"Put the gun down."

"No."

"How about I give you to the count of three?"

"How about the next word you say confirms where you are and I pull the trigger?"

The darkness sighed. "Listen, this is fun, but how 'bout we wrap it up?"

"Sounds good. We should be going anyway."

"'Fraid I can't just let you wander around."

"Point us toward the door. I'm pretty good with directions."

"Yeah, it's not that simple." The voice muttered under its breath. "Okay. Fine. Let's try something. We put them down together, okay? Then we can get somewhere safe."

"This isn't safe?"

"It might be, but that could change."

"What is this place?"

"I'll tell you all about it, but not here."

Johnathan gripped Krystal's shoulder. "Maybe we should—"

Krystal shrugged him off. "Just...give me a minute." Limited options ran through Krystal's mind. None offered much in the way of hope. "Fine." Krystal lowered her rifle. "You win."

"Good. I'm putting mine down too."

Rubber soles twisted on the tile, then came the click of something heavy and metallic being set down.

Krystal cursed under her breath and set the rifle by her feet. She rose, searching the void in front of her. "Now what?"

"Well, now—"

Sensors along the wall beeped and hummed as the building's systems rebooted. Banks of lights overhead flashed to life, but flickered as if strained. A man knelt close to the exterior wall with his muscular arms held straight in front of him. Focused brown eyes settled just above the sight of his handgun. He dressed all in black, from his tight t-shirt and double holster to his military web belt and leather boots. The twin to the gun in his hand rested on the floor next to the interior wall.

"Kick it over."

"Son of a bitch."

"*Now*."

Krystal rested her toe on the butt of the rifle and flicked it down the hall. Keeping his focus and aim, the man reached out for the rifle and slid the strap over his shoulder. Grabbing for his handgun on the floor, he holstered it, then smiled as he stood. "Better."

He took three steps back and directed to his left. "This way."

Krystal looked to the narrow hallway they had passed and opened her mouth to speak.

"No more talking. Go."

Krystal clenched her fists at her side and marched forward. Ellery and Johnathan trailed behind her and toward the dim glow emanating from an open door halfway down the hall. Once she reached the doorway, Krystal hesitated.

The man motioned forward with the gun. "Keep going."

Looking back, she narrowed her eyes, then walked into the room.

A wrap-around desk faced the entrance and occupied most of the space. On top of it, a phone and simple lamp flanked three large monitors positioned around one corner. Perched in the middle, a battery-powered lantern cast dim light over the room. A small family picture and colorful crayon drawings hung on the wall.

An older man with a wide jaw and wavy brown hair sat in a rolling leather office chair. Squinting his eyes, he frowned and pressed the screen of an oversized phone with a chunky antenna. "Stupid thing. Just work already…"

The group crowded into an empty corner of the office. The man with the gun slipped inside and rested his back against the wall beside the door. The man behind the desk looked up from the phone. His eyes brightened, and his mouth spread into a wide smile.

"Oh, hello there." He eyed each face but settled on the man with the gun. "Callen, who are your friends?"

Callen looked in Krystal's direction, but not at her. "Haven't figured that out yet."

The man in the chair scanned Ellery and Johnathan from head to toe. His smile faltered when he came to Krystal. "Hunters?"

The question went unanswered.

"Forgive me," he rose up and held out his hand, "my name is Garrett Kennington. This oasis in the wilderness is a little pet project of mine."

Ellery and Johnathan shook Garrett's hand and introduced themselves. Krystal kept her arm tight to her side.

Garrett's smile stretched, but it lacked emotion. "How did you find us?"

Krystal's gaze bore into him. "The chopper crash and the smoke."

"So, you followed the breadcrumbs."

Krystal gave a single nod.

"Speaking of which. Your camp, it's a few miles south, yes?"

Krystal hesitated, but nodded.

"We aren't the only ones to have left breadcrumbs, so to

speak. We noticed your campfire on the way in, of course." He cleared his throat and raised an eyebrow. "And, what series of events led you to be standing here with us now?"

"The door was open."

"Open?" Garrett's eyes darted to Callen.

"Well, we helped that guy, right? Then—"

Krystal's hand snapped out and smacked Ellery.

Garrett slid his phone into his pocket, then leaned forward and tilted his head. "That guy?"

Commotion from the hall interrupted the conversation. The call and response of voices were hushed, yet urgent.

"…bringing me up into this cold-ass bullshit, only to get stuck babysitting a bunch of over-privileged motherfuckers in the middle of some fucked up—" The man paused and turned to the faces watching him. He adjusted the fur hunting cap on his head.

"Linford, please." Garrett looked past him through the door.

Linford muttered and wiped at his nose. He nodded to Callen as he walked inside and moved behind Garrett. "Sorry, Mr. Kennington."

Another man stood at the door. Straight black hair tied tight behind his head, and his button-up shirt appeared one size too big. Perspiration spotted his face, and his breath came in short bursts as he scurried in and shut the door.

"Are you all right, Raymond?"

Linford leaned back against an open patch of wall. "He might have pissed his pants, but otherwise, he's fine."

"Shut it, Linford."

Garrett held up a hand. "Enough, please."

Linford crossed his arms and picked at his teeth with his tongue.

"Thank you." Garrett motioned to the man standing in front of the door. "This is Raymond Meekis, our operations manager." He then turned to Linford. "The lover of foul language here and my personal security detail, to put rather serious terms to it, is Linford, as I mentioned. Linford and Raymond, please meet Ellery, Johnathan, and…"

Krystal held her tongue, but the waiting eyes got to her soon enough.

"Krystal."

Garrett smiled. "Wonderful. Thank you, Krystal."

Krystal looked to Ray. "Operations manager of what exactly?"

Ray stammered and looked at Garrett.

Garrett raised the flat of his hand. "We offer a premier collection of experiences, custom-built to fulfill the needs of a very particular clientele." He held his hands out in front of him and moved them like he was shaping clay. "I like to think we take dreams and turn them into reality."

"That's a lot of words and little real information."

Garrett's eyes narrowed. "Let me clarify…" He cleared his throat as he moved back behind the desk. "This facility is a full-service resort. With the comfort of our guests being paramount, we offer luxury suites, a world-class spa experience, and restaurants run by award-winning chefs. I assume you've seen the main level?"

Krystal nodded.

"It's the nucleus of the operation. Games of chance like you will find nowhere else. You want high stakes? We take them into the stratosphere." Garrett reclined in his chair, folding his arms. "You may be curious about my choice in location. First off, our clients hold their privacy and security above all else. Second, to avoid certain…legal complications, it was necessary to find a local authority who was willing to work with our needs."

Ellery tilted his head and pulled at one ear. "Wait. It's like those riverboats in the south, right? The gambling, it's kind of legal, but it's not?"

Garrett smiled to his ears. "Not a bad way to put it." He turned to Krystal. "I hope that answers your questions."

Krystal showed no emotion. "Sure."

"Excellent." Garrett focused on Linford next. "Were you able to find any sign of Remo?"

"No, sir."

"Well, I think our friends here might be able to shed some light on his whereabouts." Garrett pointed to Ellery. "I believe you mentioned seeing someone."

"Uh, yeah." Ellery's eyes shifted from Krystal to meet Garrett's. "When we were walking around the building, you know, outside, we found this guy trying to get out. But there was this giant chunk of metal blocking the door, so we got it out of the way."

"And what did this…guy, look like? About my height, blue coveralls?" Garrett pulled a chain from the top of his shirt, and a wedge of glossy metal emerged. "Might have had something that looks like this?"

Ellery raised an eyebrow. "Uh…yeah. I think so."

Garrett clapped his hands. "Wonderful. What happened after you aided his exit from the facility?"

"He freaked out. Took out a gun and started shooting. We ducked inside, and the door locked."

Krystal waited for the next question. Why would someone start shooting for no reason? Instead, Garrett slid the nail of his thumb to his lips and stared at the floor. When no question came, she asked her own. "Why don't any of the doors have handles?"

Garrett scratched at his chin, then leaned his elbows onto the desk. "This facility, and every piece of equipment in it, are state of the art—beyond state of the art. Biometrics, thermal imaging, and sensors measure particulate in the air. We could tell you what you ate for lunch if we wanted to. The system connects to everything and everyone. We can limit where customers go, where employees go, down to specific doors and specific times. Total control."

Krystal tilted her head. "I sense a 'but' coming on."

Garrett settled back from the desk. "Each failsafe has a failsafe. Every eventuality was considered and prepared for, or so I thought." He frowned and waved the back of his hand. "The majority of the facility runs on solar. The backup generators are bulletproof. Trust me, I tried to prove the claim wrong. What they aren't is fireproof. Neither is the management system."

"How did the fire start?"

Garrett shot a look at Ray, but he averted his eyes. "Sabotage, I'm afraid. Terrorists exist in all areas of the world, even the most remote."

"Terrorists?"

"As I said."

"What—"

Garrett swatted Krystal's question away before she could finish. "I'm afraid we have more important matters to focus on at the moment." He turned back to Ellery. "Which exit was it?"

Krystal answered for him. "I could show you."

"I'm sure that won't be necessary." Garrett glanced sidelong at Krystal. "He mentioned something blocking a door. May I assume you made it to the far north end?" He motioned his hand in the air. "The fire, yes?"

Krystal nodded.

Garrett turned to face Callen. "There are other ways out. Why that door?"

Callen straightened his posture. "Wasn't anyone else around at that point. He could do what he wanted without being seen."

"Would you be so kind as to have a look and report back?"

"Sure." Callen pushed away from the wall. He propped Krystal's rifle in a corner away from the group, opened the door, and slipped out.

Krystal stepped forward. "We should get back to camp and get out of your way."

Standing, Garrett waved the notion off. "Nonsense. While I have no doubt that you are more than capable, it would be our honor if you would stay. We have fully prepared guest rooms with no guests." He shook an oversized gold watch down his wrist. "Besides, it's late. The sun will be down soon." A satisfied smile spread across his face. "You'll be safe here."

Krystal balled her hand into a fist and looked away.

"Well," Ellery shrugged, "I'd be okay with not spending another night in the cold."

Garrett chuckled and grabbed Ellery's shoulder. "That's the spirit, son." He turned him to face Ray. "Why don't you take our guests upstairs. Linford and I will see about getting the kitchen fired up and begin preparations for dinner."

Linford's eyes widened. "Say again?"

With his hand, Garrett directed Ellery to the door. "Go on then. You'll be taken care of, I promise."

Ray crossed his arms high over his chest. "Are you sure we shouldn't open up the staff quarters?"

Garrett shook his head. "It's important that our guests are comfortable. Besides," he locked eyes with Ray, "we wouldn't want to disturb them with any repairs still required."

Ray nodded and broke away from Garrett's steady gaze. "Good enough." He lumbered toward the door. "Follow me, please."

"Wait."

Ray stopped with his hand on the door.

Krystal motioned to Garrett. "You have a phone."

Garret's smile waned as he slowly turned to face her. "Pardon?"

"You have a satphone. I'd appreciate it if I could make a call."

Garrett cocked an eyebrow.

"Please."

"Well," Garrett pulled the phone from his pocket, "I do, but there seems to be some sort of issue at the moment." He fanned a hand at the ceiling. "Satellites and all that."

"If I don't call in, there's going to be a bunch of hostile rednecks tearing the forest apart by morning, and I'd prefer to not cause anyone any problems."

Garrett frowned. "We wouldn't want that, would we?" He held the phone out.

Krystal steadied her hand, trying not to take it too quickly. She tapped at the screen, dialed, and pressed it to her ear. The line crackled between rings, and Clint's voicemail message followed. Krystal forced sweetness when she spoke.

"Hey, Cuz, just checking in. Living the dream here. Talk to you soon. Bye."

Krystal disconnected the call and passed the phone back to Garrett. "Thank you."

"Most welcome." Garrett watched her carefully. "If there's nothing else…"

Ray pushed the door wide but stopped with his head down when Krystal spoke again.

"What about my gun?"

Garrett sighed and forced a smile. "It will be kept safe, I promise."

"It's safer with me."

Garrett clasped his hands in front of him and straightened his back. "We have strict rules, especially considering our current predicament. It will be one less thing to be concerned about if we secure it in our lockup."

Krystal scowled, staring Garrett down before moving toward the others waiting by the door.

Ray walked out to the hall without looking back. Ellery and Johnathan followed right behind him, and Krystal stomped out soon after.

Garrett rubbed at his brow and faced Linford.

Linford simply raised an eyebrow and shrugged.

SIXTEEN

Callen pushed through the door at the back corner of the building. A wide patch of trampled snow spread out past the exit with bits of torn clothing and flecks of blood littering the area. Individual footprints led away from the mess in every direction.

Circling back along the treeline, he stopped at the north end of the equipment building. The first section had buckled and collapsed in on itself. Charred skeletons of ATVs, snow removal equipment, and a tractor filled the space. Through the broken roll-up door and the haze within, he spotted two snowmobiles where there should have been four. Both were blackened and surrounded by melted plastic, and their treads fused to the concrete. At the third bay, he slipped his key into the man-door and turned it. The warped frame stopped the door from opening, but he bashed his shoulder against it until it gave.

The fire had not traveled as far as the shop, but a thick layer of soot covered everything inside. Heavy workbenches and tall toolboxes with narrow drawers lined the walls. Two snowmobiles were positioned close to the roll-up door, one with the hood forward and important looking parts on a cart beside it. A lift tucked behind the other, but it laid flat on the ground.

Ash stuck to Callen's boots, and he left clear footprints on the concrete as he walked to a cabinet at the back wall. He opened the doors wide and knelt down. Matching containers filled every surface. He pulled the bins from the bottom shelf, stacked them on the floor, then reached into the cabinet. Searching for a small, drilled hole in the back panel, Callen hooked a finger in it and pulled. He set the loose board on top of the bins.

Reaching into the cabinet the second time, he removed a black canvas bag. He flipped it over in his hands, checking for damage. Finding none, he unzipped the top and spread it out. Two holstered handguns, boxes of ammo, and a collection of sheathed knives lined one compartment. Body armor and insulated clothing filled the other side. In an end pocket, neat stacks of money and plastic identification cards wrapped in thick elastic bands, and two older cell phones in individual plastic bags.

Callen zipped the bag and stood. He slipped one of the straps over his shoulder, closed the cabinet, and wiped his hands down his pants. Turning to the still assembled snowmobile by the exit, he cleared off the gauges, then turned the key. The engine roared to life, and lights blasted the door in front of it. Callen snapped the ignition back, then pulled the key and stuck it in his pocket. He buried his bag beneath totes and tarps in the rear-mounted basket, double-checked the latch on the roll-up, then walked outside, pulling hard on the small door to close it.

SEVENTEEN

Ray led the group to the dead end where they had been found in the building. He held his wrist to the circular sensor on the wall and waited.

"Come on."

He pulled his hand away, then waved it in front again, but nothing happened.

"Guess basic means basic."

Ellery leaned around Johnathan. "What, uh, are you trying to do?"

Ray fished in his pocket. "We get these chips under our skin, a radio something-or-other. Seems they're not working right now."

Ellery pushed his way around Johnathan. "Holy shit. An RFID?"

"Uh, yeah, sounds about right." Ray slipped his key in the door and turned it with a click. Another solid click came from inside the door, and it eased open.

A toothy grin broke across Ellery's face. "That's *awesome*."

Ray shrugged. "It's just part of the gig." He retrieved the key and dropped it back into his pocket, pushed the door wide, and proceeded through it.

Johnathan held the door. "What's an RFID?"

Ellery grabbed Johnathan's arm. "Radio-frequency identification device. It's like having a key card built into your body. So cool."

Krystal filed past Johnathan. Inside the next room, she turned her eyes up.

Arcing away to the opposite corner, large triangular glass panels locked together from floor to ceiling. In the center of the room, an elaborate gold chandelier suspended from the apex. Grecian white marble statues and thick-framed oil paintings dotted the interior walls. A red velvet half-round chaise, trimmed in tufted gold, occupied most of the open space.

Dark-stained wood and marble expanded across the far wall. Shiny gold wall sconces, pale imitations of the chandelier above, lit the area behind the desk. The large, brass-framed doors serving as the entrance showed the helipad a short distance beyond. Otherwise, the room was clean, with no phones and no computer screens visible.

Ray crossed the spacious room. "I'm gonna go ahead and assume the elevators are down. My apologies, but we'll have to take the stairs." He groaned as he pulled himself up the first couple of steps. Curving around to the upper level, Ellery and Johnathan ogled the décor, taking in every detail. Krystal kept her gaze firmly on the back of Ray's head.

Once at the top, the group fanned out. The ceiling height doubled, and the room opened up like a football field. Stone turrets with inset wood doors lined the perimeter of the long walls. Krystal counted seven on each side. The end of the room narrowed and was capped in glass, with two floor to ceiling tinted windows beyond. The area between was filled with small trees, flowering bushes, and what she assumed was the movement of birds.

Ray motioned to one of the turrets. "The east-facing suites have a better view this time of year." Stepping forward, he unlocked the nearest door, then continued along to the next. "The fridges are stocked with water and champagne, please help yourself. If you'd like, I can bring up some fresh fruit to hold you over until dinner is ready." He moved on to the third room, swung the door wide, then returned to the group.

"Sorry, didn't want to yell. Everything is so damn far apart." He looked over his shoulder. "Anyway, make yourselves at home. You can get out of the rooms anytime. But to get back in, you need a key."

Krystal's expression remained flat. "We can't get a key?"

Ray hooked his thumbs in his pockets. "Unfortunately, no. With the sensors down, they're in short supply."

"Is everything automated around here?"

Ray shrugged and turned away. "The customer-facing parts are. Adds to the perceived value, or so I'm told."

"Hey, uh, Raymond?" Ellery stopped looking around enough to get his question out. "What would a night here run a guy? You know, on average?"

Ray smiled. "First off, call me Ray. Nobody calls me Raymond except Mr. Kennington and my mother. Second, and I don't mean to be presumptuous, but let's just say that it's one of those, 'if you have to ask' type of situations."

Ellery nodded. "Gotcha." His trademark grin came to his lips, and he peered at Ray from the corner of his eye. "So, which room is mine?"

Ray laughed. "Well, why don't we let the lady make the

first choice." He directed his eyes to Krystal. "Which one would you like?"

Krystal cringed at the term. "I'll take the far end."

"Good choice. I mean, the rooms are all the same, but still." Ray stepped back to guide her path with this arm. "After you."

Krystal's face stayed sober as she marched through the far door and slammed it behind her.

Ellery pointed to the closest open door. "Can I go take a look?"

Ray turned back from watching Krystal storm off. "Sure. It's all yours."

"Nice." Ellery bounced through the doorway.

Johnathan tucked his hands into his pockets and rocked on his heels. "She's something, isn't she?"

Ray forced a smile. "You'd know better than me."

Johnathan shrugged. "Yeah, I guess."

"Have you known each other long?"

"We only just met a couple days ago."

"She's the guide then?" Ray glanced behind him. "Interesting."

"Not as interesting as what's going on here." Johnathan scanned the ceiling. "How the hell did a place like this get built out in the middle of nowhere?"

"You know what they say, money talks."

"Got to be a hell of a lot of money. Must be nice."

"It's got benefits. Or so I've seen. I'm just the face."

"The face?"

"Part of the deal. The council insisted on local representation."

Johnathan looked away. "Oh. Right."

Ellery leaned out of the room, grinning ear to ear. "Holy

shit, John, you're not going to believe this place. What I thought was a window is *a TV*. The bed looks right out across the wilderness. The bathrooms are nearly as big as my apartment, *and there's two of them*."

Johnathan smiled. "Wow, that's crazy."

Ellery pulled the toque from his head and ran a hand through his matted hair. "Okay, well, I'm gonna go jump on the bed naked or something."

Johnathan raised an eyebrow and chuckled. "Okay?"

Ellery checked Ray's reaction. "Oh, sorry, I mean, I was just kidding."

Ray grinned and waved him away. "Do what you need to do. It's nice to have guests that appreciate the place."

"Okay, cool." Ellery spun and ran into his room. The door clicked shut behind him.

Johnathan shrugged. "Well, guess I'd better check this out."

Ray nodded. "I hope you enjoy it."

Johnathan walked to the remaining open door and went inside.

As the door clicked shut, the light drained from Ray's face, and his shoulders slumped. With a deep sigh, he shuffled toward the stairs and back down to the lobby.

———

Krystal set her pack down and rested her back against the door. She reached her left hand behind, searching for a lock. Finding a familiar shape, she turned the deadbolt, then slid to the floor and sat cross-legged. Krystal closed her eyes and set her hands over her head, staying that way until the voices outside faded and the last of the other room's doors closed.

After taking in and pushing out a deep breath, she opened her eyes.

A wide hall stretched away in front of her. Halfway down, arched doorways led to darkened rooms on either side. At the end, two luxurious chairs that matched the bench in the lobby and an abstract painting in a wide gold frame overlooked them. Krystal brought her knees to her chest and stood. She ran the flat of her hand along the textured wall as she walked through the open doorway to her right.

The fixture in the middle of the ceiling flickered to life, adding warm ambience more than useful light. Krystal moved around the perimeter of the room, searching for inconsistencies. Neat groups of gold coat hangers gathered on either end of long bars lining the far wall. She ran her hand across the surface and through custom shoe cubbies built in beside a cabinet with narrow shelves. She ignored her reflection in the full-length mirror as she walked past it and out of the room.

Krystal crossed the hall to the opposite space, and the plush carpet transitioned to glossy marble tile. A sideboard spanned the length of the room. On the dark wood top, a single station espresso machine perched in the middle and empty baskets, awaiting fruit or baked goods, were lined up on one end. Two wrought iron chairs flanked a breakfast table across from the sideboard. An extendable TV was mounted along the back wall, and a compact sink tucked in the corner underneath it. Finding nothing of interest, Krystal moved back into the hall.

The tips of her fingers once again searched the walls as she wove her way past the chairs in the seating area, then through the nearest en suite bathroom and walk-in closet. Next, she worked her way across the bedroom, eyes scanning every available surface, and through the second en suite on the opposite side. The motion sensor lights faded in and out as she went.

Having inspected every square inch of her accommodations, she sat on the bed, gripping the edge with both hands. Through the big window at the end of the bedroom, the treetops glowed orange and red. In the distance, nightfall charged forward, chasing the last of the daylight away. After observing the view for a time, Krystal loosened the straps securing the guards around her neck and arms. She pulled them off and set them beside her.

Still watching the sunset, her hands moved to pockets and pouches in and under her jacket. Krystal laid out knives, folding and fixed, and an expandable baton next to the guards. Looking down at the collection, she took a mental inventory, then removed a silver and black handgun and set it among them.

Krystal sniffed, then reached inside her jacket. She held her phone out in front of her. Evan's smiling face flashed across the lit screen. She swiped and scrolled to his number, but her call refused to connect. Toggling to the messages screen, her thumbs hovered while she searched for what to say. Eventually, she typed a handful of words, then waited. A red exclamation mark announced the message had failed to send. Krystal swore to herself and slammed the phone down on the bed.

Leaning her weight back on her hands, she watched the last of the color fade from the sky. Turning her attention from the window, she closed her eyes and focused on her beating heart, waiting for the images flashing across her mind to settle. Drawing in a deep breath, she opened her eyes and sat up straight.

Krystal replaced two of the knives in their respective pockets, then collected the rest in her hand as she stood. Moving around the room, she stashed the blades and the baton behind vases and on high shelves. After hiding the last in the coatroom, Krystal unzipped her jacket and dropped it on the floor. She backed up against a wall and eased herself down before stretching her tired legs out. She held the handgun on her lap, finger over the trigger guard, while focusing out the open doorway to the main hall, and waited.

EIGHTEEN

Callen stood in front of the desk and waited for Garrett to look up.

"So?"

"Nothing for sure. Looks like there was some kind of fight, but it's hard to tell what was from Remo and what could have been something else."

Garrett settled into his high-backed chair. "Speaking of which, how are things looking?"

"The fire's nearly burned itself out, but it's in the arrays. Seems to still be spreading."

Garrett huffed and focused on a bare corner of the office. "Is there anything to be done about it?"

"Hard to accomplish anything when we have no resources and no staff."

"What about the equipment shed?"

"Looks like they stole two sleds. The rest are wrecked. Not much of use in there now."

Garrett chewed a fingernail while the reality of the

situation settled in his mind. He paused and eyed Callen. "Anything else I need to know?"

"No, don't think so."

"Then go find Linford and lend a hand."

"Yes, sir."

Pivoting on his heel, Callen left the office.

Garrett resumed chewing on his nail. The color across his face darkened with each short breath. After reaching his boiling point, he snarled and slammed a closed fist on the desk.

An electronic chime filled the room. Garrett turned the screen of the satellite phone face up to see the woman's contact, calling for the third time. He silenced the phone, shoved it aside, then stormed to the door and slammed it shut. Coming back around the desk, he kicked the rolling chair into the wall.

"*Fuck.*"

Sitting against the top of the desk, Garrett closed his eyes, pushed all the air from his lungs, and crossed his arms tight.

NINETEEN

A knock at the door shocked Krystal's eyes open. She sat forward slowly, and the lights in the coatroom flickered on. Another slow knock came. She rubbed her neck, yawned, then collected the gun from the carpet beside her as she stood.

Krystal pushed a plate from the previous night's dinner away with the toe of her boot as she tucked her gun to her back. She cracked the door open. Johnathan flashed a weak smile.

"Breakfast will be ready soon."

Krystal stood in place. "Okay. Thanks." She began to close the door.

"The others, they volunteered me to come and get you. Said you'd be least upset at me for bothering you."

"Did they?"

Johnathan shrugged.

"You sure it wasn't you that said that?"

Honesty showed through Johnathan's smile. "Well, I was hoping."

"I'll be out soon."

"Okay." Johnathan cocked his head. "You all right?"

Krystal nodded. "Still waking up."

"Hey, what did you think of the—"

The door clicked shut.

"Right. Good." Johnathan stuffed his hands in his pockets and walked away.

———

Krystal lifted the covered plate from the only unoccupied chair in the circle. She placed it on her lap as she sat. The air inside the aviary was still and humid. Tiny birds perched in high branches, puffed out, side by side. A few flittered around the corners, chirping and calling out. Krystal ignored them, choosing instead to watch through the aviary's glass door to the rows of turrets.

Garrett smiled while he picked a bit of bacon from his teeth. He looked out of place in his deep blue pressed slacks and a patterned button-up shirt. "Good morning. How did you sleep?"

Krystal rested both hands on the top of the plate cover. "Fine."

"Much better than a night on the cold ground, I hope."

Krystal gave a curt nod.

"Good, I'm glad." Garrett scraped the last of the scrambled eggs from his plate and into his mouth. "I hope you don't mind us setting up in here. I thought it might be nice. Watch the sunrise and all."

"Has the transport arrived?"

Garrett gave a tired smile as he chewed. "Right to business, I like it." He wiped his mouth with a black linen napkin and placed it on his empty plate. "Later this morning.

They had some weather overnight, should be in the air soon."

"I'm sure you're anxious to get back to whatever it is you need to get back to."

Garrett shrugged. "I can only imagine how full my inbox will be, but at the moment, this is more important. The rest can wait." He motioned to Ellery and Johnathan seated across from him. "I'd like to go for a little tour after breakfast so you can properly check out the facility. It won't be as impressive as if everything were up and running, but still."

"I'd really like to get back to camp."

Garrett held up his hands. "I know, I know. Don't worry, we'll be twenty minutes, thirty tops. In fact, why don't we do that now? You stay and enjoy your breakfast." He looked to Ellery and Johnathan. "Gentlemen?"

Ellery jammed the last corner of toast into his mouth and nodded as he swallowed.

Johnathan set his fork on his plate. "Ready when you are."

"Excellent." Garrett stood and raised a finger. "Oh, I need to grab something from the office. I'll meet you in the lobby in five minutes?"

"Sure."

"Wonderful. Thank you." Garrett stood and lifted a thin jacket from the back of his chair, flipped it over his shoulder, and walked through the aviary door.

Krystal removed the cover from her plate. Picking out a halved strawberry, she popped it in her mouth, then replaced the lid. "Once you guys are done wasting time, we get the hell out of here, got it?"

"It's just a quick tour." Ellery looked to Johnathan and back to Krystal. "It's not that big a deal, is it?"

"It is to me."

"Why don't we just have them drop us off at camp, or better yet, maybe they can get us back to the city? Hell, any city."

"No."

"Why not?"

Krystal's eyes searched around the ceiling perimeter. "Because I don't trust them."

"But look at this," Ellery gestured his arms around the room, "they've set us up for the night, fed us—"

"You think just because someone is nice to you, it means you can trust them with your life?"

"Well, I mean…"

"No." Krystal glanced through the door and lowered her voice. "There's a lot of weird shit happening here, and it baffles me why you two aren't more concerned. Go on your stupid tour. Do not say anything beyond what they already know. Keep your mouths shut about Darby, and especially about the truck being gone."

Johnathan broke his eyes away. "Oh…"

Krystal leaned forward. "What did you do?"

"Nothing." He scratched behind one ear. "Except…we might have shared a little too much when we were talking at dinner last night."

"Dinner?"

"Well, yeah. Just because you didn't join us doesn't mean we had to stay locked in our rooms."

Krystal groaned. "Oh, for fuck's sake."

"We had a couple drinks and got to chatting. That's all."

Krystal held up her palm. "Okay. Enough." Rechecking the door, she noticed Callen and Linford cresting the top of the stairs at the end of the long hall. "Try not to get into it again."

"Okay. Sorry."

The group stayed quiet until Callen and Linford joined them inside the aviary.

Callen stood at the glass wall and crossed his arms over his black vest. A silent walkie-talkie dangled from his belt, the lit screen scanning through the channels. "Mr. Kennington is ready for you."

Johnathan snuck a glance at Krystal. "Okay, thanks."

Ellery cleared his throat and followed Johnathan out the door.

Linford stepped into the aviary and slumped down on the chair across from Krystal. He spread his legs wide and interlaced his fingers over his stomach. "How was breakfast?"

"Not hungry."

"Shit." Linford pushed the rim of his fur hat higher over his brow. "I worked hard on that."

"Sorry."

"It's all right. If you ain't hungry, you ain't hungry."

The conversation paused as they watched each other.

"Pretty crazy, all this shit goin' on."

"More than a little."

"So, you guys seriously just out hunting and found this place?"

Krystal nodded.

"You must be serious about it."

Krystal nodded again.

Linford pulled the hat from his head, held it out in front of him while he ran a hand over his short-cropped black hair. "You know, that's how I got this. Shot the little bastard myself."

Krystal raised her eyebrow. "Really?"

Linford gave a wide, toothy grin. "Naw. I ordered it online."

Krystal frowned and looked away from him.

"It wasn't fuckin' cheap though, I'll tell you that." Linford flopped the hat back onto his head and adjusted it with both hands. "Hangin' out all day in the middle of nowhere, crawlin' around in snow and shit, ain't my idea of a good time."

"Seems you've made some interesting life choices, if that's the case."

"Hey, this ain't what I signed up for. On a normal day, if you don't look outside, you'd never know you're about as far away from civilization as it gets. Got Wi-Fi, whatever food you want, whatever drink you want. Don't get much better."

"How nice for you." Krystal kept her eyes high at the ceiling.

Linford laughed. "Look at this one." He leaned back toward Callen and motioned at Krystal with his thumb. "You weren't kidding, were you?"

Callen focused on the stairway at the other end of the building. "I tried to warn you."

With a smile, Linford eyed Krystal up and down. "It's all good."

Krystal met Linford's gaze and held back a sneer. "What is it you do here? Can't imagine you're the pretty face."

"Naw, that's my man Callen's job over there." Linford flexed his bicep. "I'm the muscle."

Krystal muttered under her breath. "Super."

Linford draped one arm over the top of the chair. "Important people need someone who has their back. Simple as that."

"Seems to me that if you aren't doing anything wrong, you don't need anyone watching your back."

"Ah," Linford wagged a finger, "not true. Doesn't matter if you done wrong or not. Just having more than someone else can make you an enemy."

Krystal twisted her lips and gave a slight nod. "Maybe."

"It's fucked up, but it's the world we live in."

Lifting the lid from the plate, Krystal grabbed another strawberry. "If you say so."

TWENTY

The flat soles of Garrett's dress shoes clicked on the tile as he walked through an opening in the wall. He unzipped his jacket, flipped the leather satchel strung over his shoulder to his back, and held his arms straight out from his sides. "Gentlemen, welcome to the main attraction."

He stood in front of the open kitchen with his hands on his hips. "No expense was spared, as you can see. We fly in fresh ingredients daily, and everything is made from scratch. Our chefs are at the top of their industry, though I am not at liberty to name names. We are nothing if not serious about our ability to maintain confidentiality. Only the best for our guests, of course. Mind you, the staff offerings are nothing to turn your nose up at."

Garrett wove his way around the dining tables and the partition of tall tropical plants. Ellery kept Garrett's pace. Johnathan trailed behind, pinching leaves between his thumb and pointer finger to confirm they were real.

Next, they stopped in the middle of the casino floor. "Games of chance," Garrett swept his hand toward the TV's lining the wall, "and games of sport. We offer it all, including access to exclusive events from around the globe." He watched Johnathan wander to the dome at the back of the space.

Johnathan pointed his hand and turned to Garrett. "What about that?"

"Ah." Garrett pressed his hands flat together. "Another piece of the immersive experience. What is better than being up close and personal, but at the same time, safe from any…" he waved a hand, "repercussions."

Johnathan peered down through the glass, and the floor fell away. Tracks in the concrete walls extended beneath the floor and acted as guides for the platform, hiding in the shadows.

"Fighting. You host fights."

Garrett raised his chin. "Pardon?"

Johnathan ran a knuckle down the glass, tracing spatter on the inside. "That's what you do here. Like, MMA or something?"

Garrett's eyes narrowed. "Yes. Something like that."

"You know," Johnathan stepped back from the glass. "I don't understand what people see in it. Why people consider it a sport."

"Isn't that what all sport is? Conflict. A fight for survival. Everyone loves violence in one form or another."

Johnathan brushed his hands together, then returned them to his pockets. "I'm not so sure about that."

Garrett shrugged. "The world is big enough for all sorts of opinions." A smile crept across his lips and lit up his eyes. "Besides, it's surprising how many lines can be bent and how easy it is to cater to our most basic instincts when there's money to be made." He turned away and held out a hand in the direction of the service entrance. "Perhaps it's time we continue?"

Garrett moved away from the stairwell that led to the staff level and stepped into a circle of light. Ellery and Johnathan came around and stood in front of him. In the distance, one door closed, and then a few seconds later, another opened.

Ellery glanced sideways. "There's someone else down here?"

"Oh." Garrett leaned over. "Just Raymond making sure the rooms are clear, I imagine."

Garrett focused beyond them on a deep cinderblock wall. "You know what?" He checked his watch. "This level is a bit boring anyway. It's mostly rooms for the staff and storage. Why don't we make one last extra special stop?"

"You sure? I mean, this is cool as hell, but Krystal was pretty anxious to get going."

Garrett swatted Ellery's comment away. "She'll be fine, I promise. This will only take a minute."

Repositioning the strap of his leather satchel over his shoulder, Garret lifted the key from his pocket. He walked around the cinderblock wall and past a set of wide elevator doors. Pausing in front of a single unmarked door with a bold restricted access sign on the front, he smiled and waved the pair over. "It's a rare treat to see the basement."

Ellery scratched at his temple and combed his fingers through the hair on the side of his head. "Aren't we already in the basement?"

"Forgive me. It is the sub-basement, to be more specific." Garrett unlocked the door and pushed it wide. "Come on, this'll be great."

Ellery and Johnathan shot each other a brief glance, then followed along.

Narrow concrete steps led them down at a steep angle. Garrett's voice echoed behind him. "This is one of those situations where taking the elevator is a more pleasant experience."

The clicking of boots quieted as they reached the bottom step and moved into an open area. Garrett slid his key into the wall, and a large panel released, swinging back on heavy hinges. Red lights flashed on either side of the door. "Don't worry, it's just making sure we know the power is out."

He freed a similar door a short distance inside and stepped through.

Ellery stuck his head across the threshold, holding the wall with one hand. "What is this exactly?"

Garrett faced his guests. "This, gentlemen, is the whole reason we're here. The idea that powers this rather lucrative dream." He walked up to a heavy steel barred door set into a cinderblock wall to their right. With the key from his pocket, he unlocked it and pushed it wide open.

Johnathan nudged Ellery forward and stood beside him. "What's that smell?"

Ellery pinched his nose. "It's pretty bad."

Garrett breathed in deep. "Oh. You're right. It has been a couple days since the cleaning crew has come around. Good thing this level is on a separate ventilation system than those above." He set his satchel down beside the door. "Come on in, you need to see this."

Ellery took hesitant steps forward to stand beside Garrett. As he entered, Johnathan scanned the space. Only a few banks of lights above were lit, and acoustic panels covered the rest of the ceiling. Opposite the bottom of the stairs, two large cargo elevator doors hid in the shadows of the low light.

Down the long room to his left, a large black metal box

was tucked into the corner. Similar to a small shipping container, a square door sunk into its face, well off the floor. Metal pipes sprouted from a complicated control panel and converged along the wall.

Two gurneys with metal rollers built into the tops sat at an angle next to the box. Their height matched the door. Johnathan had watched enough crime dramas to get the idea. Across from the incinerator, the opposite wall was clad in white. A wide, rectangular door with a pull handle had a sign on the front that read 'freezer'.

Johnathan turned back to the cinderblock wall. Bleak light cast through the barred door and lit the clouded windows on either side with an ominous glow. Through the opening, lines of low cages reached the far wall, and thick stains on the concrete buzzed with flies. Garrett walked along the front of each row, flicking latches as he went.

"Construction of this facility started well before the infection was released upon the world, but I shouldn't need to explain how much things have changed since then. You'd be hard-pressed to find someone who hasn't been affected by it, directly or not. It changed people. It made them angry. That anger, and the repercussions of the event, led us in new and interesting directions."

Garrett continued to the second row as he motioned the two men further in. Ellery stopped short, just past the barred door, but Johnathan walked in toward the cages.

"What people want when they're angry is revenge. In the months after the initial incident, many searched for ways to exact that revenge. Some had better luck than others, but eventually, even the most successful fell." Garrett waved a hand. "The rule of law and such."

Johnathan knelt and looked across the line of cages and to

the bundles of gray fabric balled up in each. Holding his hand over his face, he eyed the thick, black mess oozing down the fronts. The air smelled of burned copper.

"I've done very well in life by noticing opportunities and filling needs. That's exactly what I've done here. The facility, while not easy, wasn't the hard part. The process, supply lines, and secure transport, those were a challenge. But I love a good challenge, so we figured it out."

Garrett faced the cages but stepped back.

"Those early days were glorious. We were booked solid for months. The appetite for the battle over life and death was insatiable. As with most things, soon, it wasn't enough." Garrett took another step back. "I hired the best genomic and virology specialists that money could buy. The scientists took the pathogen, kept the best parts, and turned the rest up to eleven."

Johnathan reached out for the dark stain. A single shaky finger hovered above it.

"So much effort. It's a shame that things turned out the way they did."

The lights flickered. Garrett raised an eyebrow and glanced at the ceiling. "That's not good."

Hopping through the threshold, he slammed the barred door.

Ellery spun with wide eyes. Bolting forward, he grabbed at the bars. "What the hell?"

Garrett retrieved the satchel from the ground. "I'm really sorry the two of you got caught up in this, but that's the way it goes sometimes." He turned and walked toward the dark end of the space.

"What are you doing?"

"Damage control." Garrett stopped a few steps later.

"Wait, is that right?" He stared at the ceiling with one eyebrow raised, then moved on. "Anyway, doesn't matter."

Garrett hummed a cheerful tune as he crossed the rest of the room, paying no attention to the shaking metal door or cries for help. He set the satchel next to the incinerator and knelt beside it. With the top of the satchel pressed back, he reached in with both hands and eased out a clay brick. A series of wires protruded from the top of a simple electronic panel. He moved to the gurneys, set it on one of them, then rolled it clear of the wall just as the lights went out for good.

TWENTY-ONE

Krystal sat back in the chair and attempted to look comfortable. She listened to the building and to Callen and Linford's hushed conversation across the room. Neither offered anything new, so she checked her watch for the third time in as many minutes.

The room dimmed. Krystal focused through the glass wall to the nearest lamp shade. Flickering, it darkened for a heartbeat, then glowed back to life. Slowly getting to her feet, she looked to Callen and Linford as their conversation trailed away. Linford surveyed the ceiling in the main room. Callen watched Krystal.

"I'd like to go find my friends now."

Callen considered Krystal's statement and turned to Linford. "Probably a good idea if you go check in."

Linford nodded and unclipped the walkie from his belt. "Mr. Kennington, everything okay down there?"

He released the button and stared off into space as he waited. No response came. He snuck a glance at Callen and lifted the walkie to his chin. "Boss? You there?" He scanned the room as the lights flickered once more, then went out.

"Shit." Linford twisted a knob on the top of the walkie and pressed the button again. "Ray? Where you at? *Ray?*"

Nothing but static.

Linford returned the walkie to his belt. "Where's he supposed to be?"

"Said he needed to do final checks on the staff level."

Linford looked toward the opposite end of the building and the staircase to the lobby. "I'm gonna head to the main level, check out front, and work my way back."

Callen nodded. "I'll head down from this end and find Ray. We'll meet you in the middle."

"I'm coming with you."

Linford and Callen spun around, having nearly forgotten Krystal was there.

Callen tilted his head. "What?"

Krystal stepped forward. "I'm coming with you."

"No."

Krystal narrowed her gaze and stood her ground.

"It's better if you stay here."

"Either I come with you now, or I wander around and see what I can find on my own."

Callen ground his teeth and stared.

Linford smacked Callen's shoulder with the back of his hand on his way out the door. "Good luck."

Callen sighed. "Yeah. Thanks."

TWENTY-TWO

Ray leaned back, facing the ceiling with his hands interlocked over his head. Lazy smoke trailed from the cigarette hanging loose on his lips. His eyelids bobbed as they threatened to close, and his breathing became shallow.

The lights outside the room faltered once, then again. Ray peeled one eye open and watched through the door. Shadows cut across the design of the muted wallpaper. They swallowed it all together when the lights went out.

He sighed. "Shit. Not again." Groaning, he sat up straight. "Can't get five damn minutes to relax, can I?"

Ray wiped the end of the cigarette on his pant leg, then brushed away the residual ash. He set the butt end back between his lips and pushed himself up from the chair. Holding one hand out in front of him, Ray eased his way out of the room. The blue screen of his walkie-talkie flashed silently as he guided himself through the dark toward the back of the building.

TWENTY-THREE

Callen skimmed down the staircase, almost as fast as if he was falling. He held his gun, and the bright, focused beam of a flashlight aimed ahead of his feet. Krystal stayed close behind, one hand grazing the wall as they descended into hazy air that held a tinge of burned electrical wire.

They flashed past the door where the hunting group had entered the building. At the bottom of the next set of stairs, Callen's pace slowed. He moved to the middle of the passageway along the short side of the building. A cargo elevator, with only a down button, had a smaller metal door propped open next to it. Callen inched toward the door with his back to the wall. Scanning from left to right, he turned an ear to the narrow concrete steps leading down into the darkness. Faint but urgent noises echoed from the level below.

Krystal stood a few paces behind Callen. "Where does that go?"

Callen pinched his lips tight and pushed air out through his nose. "I need you to stay here."

"Until I find my friends, I'm not staying anywhere."

"Friends, huh?"

Krystal did not respond.

"Christ." Callen raised his gun and stepped through the door. "Don't say I didn't warn you."

The stairs curved in a tight arc. Krystal kept one hand at her back as they descended, taking each step much slower than they had from the upper level. She emerged from the stairwell and stood at Callen's left. They both stared through the opening of a decontamination chamber as voices called out beyond.

"Hello? Anybody?"

"*Help us, please.*"

Krystal spoke low. "Ellery and Johnathan." She managed one step forward.

Callen reached out and grabbed the back of her coat. "No."

She smacked his hand away. "What do you mean, no?"

"Not a good idea."

"Very little of what I've agreed to here has been a good idea, but I made a promise to keep them safe."

Callen darted his eyes toward the door. "Yeah, well, I can guarantee this isn't something you planned for."

Metal hinges groaned in the darkness.

"Hey. *Hey.*"

"What the...*no.*"

Words devolved to panicked screaming. Strained breathing and skin slapping against the concrete floor echoed out. Krystal felt the impact of each kick and cracking bone in her gut.

She snatched the flashlight from Callen's hand and pushed past him as the cries faded to whimpers and then into silence.

She stopped in the open space and directed the beam through the wide double barred doors.

A big man with a sagging belly and thick forearms pushed himself up on one knee before standing. He stared Krystal down, towering over her, while a slow smile crept across his blood-flecked face. Johnathan laid on the ground behind him, his scalp matted with gore, and the clothes covering his broken body stained red. At the edge of the flashlight's glow, Ellery's foot shuddered as his boots slid across the floor and disappeared into the shadows.

The big man's eyes twitched when Callen arrived at Krystal's side. The haze of light revealed others with fierce eyes and blood-stained hands milling around behind the big man.

Krystal glared at him, rage rising in her throat. She moved forward, but Callen held her back. He shook his head, then stepped in front of her and raised the sight of his gun square between the man's eyes. His finger tensed over the trigger, but froze when a click sounded behind them.

"No sudden movements, please."

Krystal spun around to see a gun pointed at the back of Callen's head.

Garrett gave a reverse nod. "You certainly have an issue with following directions, don't you?" He cleared his throat and adjusted his stance. "Callen, would you be so kind as to put your gun on the ground?"

Callen hesitated, then turned his gun sideways and leaned down to place it on the floor beside him.

"Now the other one."

Callen sighed, then repeated the process after taking his second gun from its holster.

"What about you?"

Krystal's body tensed. "I don't have anything."

Garrett smiled. "Doubtful." He motioned to her belt. "Knife. Or knives?"

Krystal pulled open the hem of her jacket and slipped a folded blade from its sheath. Maintaining eye contact, she held the other hand out, fingers splayed, and lowered it to her leg. She dug into a pocket at her thigh, pulled out another knife, and dropped both in front of her. "That's it."

Garrett licked at his dry lips. "I suppose I'll take your word for it. Callen, you can turn around now."

Callen turned to face Garrett. "I'm surprised you didn't just shoot me in the back."

Garrett smiled wide. "Let's be rational, Callen. I'm no killer. I have people do that for me. People like you." He motioned to the wall opposite the stairwell. "Start walking. Door number one, please."

Callen stared at the doors, but did not move.

Garrett waved his gun. "Go on."

Callen scowled and moved in front of the cargo door on the left. Krystal stood behind him.

"Callen, would you be so kind?"

"Not sure I follow."

"Of course, you do." The barrel of Garrett's gun swayed between Callen and Krystal. "How about I give you five seconds?"

Callen stayed firm.

"Five. Four."

Krystal shot Callen a glance.

"Three. Two."

Callen's nostrils flared. "*Fine.*" He pulled the chain from around his neck, lifted it over his head, and held the key out.

"Open the door."

Stepping in front of the small door, Callen inserted the key and twisted it. The door unlatched and cracked open.

"Now, throw me the key."

Callen sneered at Garrett. "You're gonna kill us too?"

Garrett shook his head. "I haven't killed anyone."

Callen pointed to the glossy mess behind the barred doors. "What the fuck do you call that?"

Garrett shrugged. "Maybe they should have been better prepared."

"You sick piece of shit."

"Off you go." Garrett flashed a nervous smile.

Callen balled his hands into fists and planted his feet.

"Ah, ah, ah. You won't make it. I promise."

"*Fuck you.*" Callen threw the key at Garrett's feet, then pulled the door back and stormed through.

Krystal took one step to follow, but stopped and focused on Garrett. She held his gaze until his smile faltered, then moved to catch up with Callen.

Garrett skittered forward, grabbed the edge of the door, and slammed it. He lowered his gun and tilted his head back. Drawing in a deep breath, he let it slowly drift out.

In the dark, someone tested the barred door, then shuffling noises settled to silence. Garrett blinked his eyes, but they would not adjust to the lack of light. Patting his jacket pockets, he located and pulled out his cell phone. He swiped to the flashlight app and, in the unfocused light, collected the guns and knives scattered across the floor.

TWENTY-FOUR

Callen screamed out and launched at the door with the flat of his boot. Chest heaving, he staggered back and stood with his hands clenched at his sides.

Krystal backed into a corner with her arms crossed. "You done now?"

Callen half-turned his head and glared at her. Without answering, he took the flashlight from her and walked to a narrow break in the concrete wall. He gripped the flashlight between his teeth, reached high, then pulled himself up a concealed ladder built into the surface. Krystal dropped her hands and rushed after him.

Boots clanged on metal rungs. Krystal fumbled along until she caught the rhythm. The space at her back widened as they climbed. Chilled air burned her lungs, and the smell of earth overwhelmed. Just as she considered the journey might go on forever, Callen stopped. Krystal halted a moment later, then backed down one rung as she looked up.

Callen grunted and strained as the creak of cold metal hinges echoed around them. A final shove flooded the shaft with bland daylight. He squeezed himself out, then braced the door and waited for Krystal to emerge. With her feet on solid ground, she wiped her hands down the front of her jacket. Sporadic snow fell as she absorbed her surroundings.

"This isn't good."

"You don't know the half of it." Callen checked behind him. "And keep your voice down."

Razor wire capped a tall chain-link fence around them. From the outside, Krystal had not noticed the red stained tracks in the packed snow around the perimeter. Questions flared in her mind, but she kept them to herself, unsure if she wanted confirmation of the truth.

"What now?"

"We need to get out of here."

"No shit. How do we do that?"

Callen faced the platform perched high between the enclosures and pointed.

TWENTY-FIVE

Garrett bent over the gurney, holding his cell phone out to illuminate his work. When he finished securing wires into the top of the malleable, gray brick, he set the phone down with the light facing the ceiling. Turning away, he kicked the satchel at his feet. The guns and knives inside clinked together as it tumbled over. Garrett pushed the bag closer to the cart with the tip of his shiny shoe, then walked around the far side of the incinerator.

He returned with a long pipe wrench hanging at his side. It hit the concrete with a thud when he set it down to adjust his grasp. Raising the wrench over his head, he brought it down on the thickest pipe strapped to the wall. He winced as the clang echoed away. Repositioning his feet, he swung again.

"Come on."

Drawing in a sharp breath, he lifted the wrench higher.

"*Come on.*"

The wrench rebounded away as the pipe cracked and split open. The smell of rotten eggs washed over Garrett. Blocking his face with one arm, he pressed a button on the small screen attached to the brick of explosive, then bent to lift the satchel as he darted away.

At the door to the decontamination chamber, he paused. The corners of his lips twitched, and soon, his smile grew wide and obscene. He stepped back and stole a glance at the barred doors before he tucked his hand in his pocket and walked toward it. When he brought his hand out, Callen's key hung from his fingertips.

"You've got ten minutes. Let's see if all those scientists were money well spent."

Garrett flipped the key through the bars. It hit the floor and slid to a stop at the big man's feet. The man looked down, then back to Garrett. Garrett gave a crude salute and turned to run upstairs.

When he reached the top, he was short of breath. Guiding the last door closed, he stopped it before it latched.

"Mr. Kennington?"

Garrett spun and held his arms out, eyes wide. "Raymond. Jesus Christ." He held a hand over his pounding heart. "You scared the living hell out of me."

"Sorry." Ray looked around Garrett to the door. "Everything okay? Sort of smells like propane."

Garrett smiled. "Sure, sure it is. Oh," he pulled the satchel forward, "I've got something for you. Let me see here…"

Garrett rooted through the contents of the bag until he settled on one of the matching handguns at the bottom. "Here we go."

Pulling the gun free, he aimed it at Ray's chest and pulled the trigger twice. Ray crumpled to the ground as the air escaped his lungs.

"Damnit." Garrett scanned the space. He raised the gun, pointed it to his left without looking, and fired it twice more.

Next, he angled it toward his side. Garrett hesitated, then raised it to his opposite shoulder. Closing his eyes, he squeezed the trigger one last time.

"Christ almighty."

Garrett dropped the gun back in the satchel, then heaved it along the hall. Gripping his bleeding shoulder, he slid down the nearest wall. "Wow. That really stings."

Linford burst out of the long hall with his gun raised, scanning in all directions. He knelt beside Garrett but kept his focus on Ray. "What the fuck happened here?"

Garrett winced. "The woman. She grabbed one of Callen's guns. She…" He gestured toward Ray, lying prone on the ground.

"Where did she go? What about the other two?"

"I'm not sure. Callen went after them." Garrett reached out for Linford's shoulder. "They were in on it the whole time, Linford. They got into the basement."

Linford leaned to look at the access door beside the elevator and drew in a short breath. "Yeah, that's not good." He listened. "Are they still down there?"

Garrett lowered his eyes and shook his head.

Linford wedged his hand under Garrett's good arm and hoisted him to his feet. "Let's go.

"You don't think…"

"I ain't about to hang around and find out." Linford cast a concerned glance at Ray, then dragged Garrett away.

TWENTY-SIX

Krystal zipped her jacket. "So, let's go then."

Callen shielded his eyes with his hand and scanned the nearby trees. "Yeah, just hold up a minute."

He walked toward the opposite corner of the enclosure and behind a thin tree. Reaching up, he tugged something free from a low hanging branch.

"You're shitting me."

Callen stalked over to Krystal with an axe in his hand. Krystal looked around the open area, studying the covered elevator shaft and retracing steps in her mind. When she snapped back to attention, she focused hard on the details of the enclosure. "What the fuck is wrong with you people?"

"Where would you like me to start?"

Fishing under the back of her coat, Krystal took out her gun.

Callen's chin dropped. "You've had a gun this whole fuckin' time? You could have just dealt with him. Instead, you let that prick push us out here?" Callen tightened his grip on the axe.

"In case your short-term memory is faulty, he had a gun at our backs the whole time. How exactly did you expect me to get the upper hand in that situation?" Krystal scowled and turned away. "Plus, how the hell was I supposed to know what we were getting into?"

Callen threw his free hand up. "After what you saw in there, what gave you the impression this would be better?"

In the distance, a branch shifted, and a clump of snow fell to the ground.

Krystal sighed and raised her eyes to the platform. "You're sure that's the only way?"

"This might come as a surprise, but the point of this place is to keep people in. Not like there's a door to walk out of."

"Fine. Then we'd better get moving."

TWENTY-SEVEN

Linford guided Garrett into the office and closed the door behind them. He stood flat against the wall and watched as Garrett fought with the switches of the battery-powered lanterns on the desk.

"How long until our ride arrives?"

"Half hour or so. Assuming it's still on schedule."

"Wonderful." Garrett set his phone face down after checking the screen. He opened and closed the desk's top drawer, then opened the one below and pulled out the satellite phone. Seeing the seven missed calls, he set it down on top of his own.

"We should get your shoulder wrapped up."

Garrett glanced at the dark stain running down his sleeve. "It's fine. Just a, ah, flesh wound."

"If you're sure."

"Well…" Garrett winced, sliding his shoulder out of his jacket. "Maybe that isn't such a bad idea."

"Key?"

"Right." Garrett fetched a key from his pocket and held it out.

Linford stepped forward, retrieved the key, and took one of the lanterns. "Be right back."

He stuck his head out the door and listened, then turned toward two doors facing each other at the end of the hall. One door led to the big reception desk in the lobby. Linford slipped the key into the lock of the other and eased it open.

He held the lantern high and guided it from corner to corner. The light reflected across stainless steel cabinets and drawers, a backless rolling stool, and an examination table. Moving inside, he pulled on random doors and drawers until he found bandages, tape, and a pair of short, pointed scissors. He grasped them all in his free hand and went back to the office.

Garrett lowered the satphone from his ear and put it on the desk when Linford returned.

"Anything?"

Garrett frowned and shook his head.

Linford moved to the end of the desk and dropped the stack of medical supplies. "You need me to take a look?"

"I'm fine." Garrett unbuttoned the cuff of his blood-soaked sleeve, then the first few buttons down from his collar. He pushed his shirt off of his shoulder and gazed down. "Oh, that's not good." He poked the edge of the entrance wound. Torn and swollen tissue oozed red. Grabbing a short stack of gauze, he pressed it to his arm, then reclined in the chair and shut his eyes.

Linford snipped off four lengths of tape and pasted them over the edges of the gauze.

"Water?"

"What?"

Garrett coughed. "Is there any water?"

"Oh, I think Ray…I mean, should be some in the fridge under the desk."

Garrett found the small fridge underneath, hooked his shoe on the door, and flicked it open. Scanning the contents, he sighed and let the door close. "Oh well, it can wait, I guess."

Linford shrugged and rested against the wall.

The floor shook, and a dull rumble reverberated up the hall.

"The fuck was that?"

"I have no idea. You'd better make sure the door is locked." Garrett turned away to button his shirt and hide his growing smile.

TWENTY-EIGHT

Krystal marched along the treeline, close to the chain-link fence, with her gun aimed low. Callen stalked behind her with the axe dangling at his side. His gaze traced their tracks in the snow, then along the path ahead.

Krystal stopped next to the tower and looked up through the chain-link. "This isn't a good idea."

"You have a better one?"

"No, but that doesn't mean this is the best option. Maybe we can chop a tree down and use it to climb out."

Callen watched all around them. "Shit, might as well go running around screaming and waving our arms, too."

Krystal gritted her teeth. "You know what? I'm sick of your shitty attitude. You want to do this? Fine. But I'm telling you, it isn't going to work."

Callen propped the axe against the fence. "I guess we'll see." Reaching up, he laced his fingers through the wire and pulled.

Krystal scowled, jammed her gun into the back of her waistband, then slipped off her jacket and gripped the collar in her teeth. She looped her fingers, planted her foot against the fence, and shimmied up.

In the blink of an eye, she caught up to Callen as he strained to gain altitude. She did not look in his direction or say a word when she pulled ahead. Just as she slowed to confirm her lead, a heavy mass crashed into the fence below. Her arms jolted as her boot lost its purchase and slipped away. With the second impact, Callen lost his grip.

"*Shit.*"

He swung his arm up, but cold fingers missed their mark, and he dropped.

Spinning, Callen aimed his boot into a snarling face. The woman below him fell sideways with a bloodied cheek. He hit the ground in a crouch and reached for the axe. As he jumped back, he pulled the collar of his shirt over his nose. A thin and dirty man charged at him from the back of the enclosure. Dark gore ran from his mouth, staining a once-white t-shirt, and steam trailed behind him in the brisk air. Callen struck him in the chest with the aft end of the axe. When the man slumped to his knees, he buried the sharp end into the crown of the man's skull.

Callen worked the axe free, then forced the butt end of the handle skyward, catching another attacker in the jaw. He spun and stuck the axe deep into their neck. The attacker gurgled as their legs lost their strength and buckled to the ground.

A heavy-set woman ran from the trees with her arms outstretched. Callen managed to deflect, but the gangly man charging in behind her caught him low around his waist and pinned him to the ground. Callen braced the axe's handle against the man's throat in an attempt to pry him off.

A gunshot rang out. One of the man's eyes caved into his head and blew out of the back. As he collapsed, the heavy woman rolled over and rose onto her hands and knees, crawling toward Callen. She opened her mouth to scream, but the second gunshot created a sizable hole in her forehead. Her body relaxed and fell into a pool of gore-stained snow.

Krystal kept a rigid stance and sighted in the direction the two aggressors had emerged from. Crunching footfall in the snow and angry growling echoed through the trees. Callen stood on trembling legs and held the axe at the ready.

Vibration from the ground shook tree branches, showering them with snow. The earth between the enclosure and the main building cracked and heaved, rose to near eye level, then toppled into a giant sinkhole. Through the tinted windows on the end of the building, a fireball flashed. Sections of the nearby chain-link fence slackened and bowed, and the corners of the enclosure buckled inward.

Krystal knelt, aiming into the trees. She fired three successive shots, each dropping a body to the snow. She snatched her jacket from the ground beside her and got to her feet. Scanning for movement, she backed away. Callen looked to the chain-link and followed.

At the lowest section of the fence, Krystal holstered her gun. "Give me a boost."

Callen opened his mouth to argue, but held his tongue. He dropped the axe and interlocked his fingers. Krystal tossed her jacket up to hang over the razor wire, then set one boot in Callen's hands and jumped.

She caught the edge, worked one arm over, and climbed up to straddle the fence. "Okay, your turn."

Callen looked up to Krystal and shook his head. "Easier said than done." He collected the axe and took a few steps back.

"Think you can hook it?"

"Maybe."

He wiped fresh snow from his hand, switched the axe over, then cleaned off the other. After drawing in a deep breath, he charged forward. The axe clanged as metal met with metal, and it caught the top of the fence. Hanging from the handle, Callen tensed before repositioning one hand to the middle. He drew in and pushed out another breath, then swung his other hand further up.

Krystal hooked her boots along the top of the fence and leaned down with her hand extended.

Callen's arms began to shake. "Ready?"

"Do it."

His hand shot out, and they locked onto each other's forearms. Krystal pulled as the fence bowed from the shifting weight.

"Ever think about eating a salad once in a while?"

Callen grunted as his foot caught the top of the fence on his second attempt. "Vegetables are what food eats."

Krystal allowed a smile as they both sat up on the edge of her jacket, gulping for air. "You're not wrong."

She brought one leg up and perched on top of the fence. Holding a length of bunched-up razor wire, she tucked her legs, spun, and hopped down. Krystal's back hit the outside section of the chain-link, and she slid to land on the broken ground.

"Hey."

Callen leaned over and looked down.

Krystal faced up, shielding her eyes. "Don't forget my jacket."

He saluted. "Yes, boss."

In one motion, Callen turned to the outside and pulled his legs up to balance on the top of the fence. He shook

Krystal's jacket free of the coiled wire and tossed it to her. Next, Callen reached out to support himself so he could shift his footing. When he brought his first foot closer to the edge, it slipped, and he pitched forward. Callen tucked his limbs as his body rolled and smacked against the fence before sliding down. At the bottom, he laid flat on his back and groaned.

Krystal stood over him with her hands on her hips. "Smooth."

Callen rose on his knees and brushed snow from his clothes. "Thanks."

"I think your friends only gave it an eight-point-five, though."

Callen raised an eyebrow, then looked behind him.

Infected clustered along the fence. Rancid hot breath mixed with the steam rising from their skin. They watched with intent, predators waiting for their prey to take one fatal step closer.

Callen winced as he stood. "I'll try harder next time."

Krystal shrugged her jacket on and zipped it partway. She shook her arms at her side and waited for the chill to subside. "How many are in there?"

"Usually a dozen at a time."

"Shit."

"Don't know if that's what we need to worry about at the moment."

Thick smoke seeped from breaks in the frozen soil. The pristine, flat walls of the building buckled and threatened to crumble. Krystal turned away from the treeline and side-stepped to level ground. Tucked in the rear corner of the cleared land, fumes billowed from behind a wood fence.

"What's that?"

Callen followed the direction of her gaze. "Propane. It's for the incinerator."

"Not a good thing that it's smoking then?"

"No."

Krystal looked to the building. "How do we get back inside?"

"Why do you want to go back in?"

"Just tell me how."

"Kennington took my only key."

"Yeah, I know."

Callen shrugged.

"Guess that means we're going through the front door." Krystal walked south along the closest side of the building.

"Wait."

She stopped and glanced behind her. "What now?"

Callen stuck a thumb over his shoulder. "This way."

Krystal looked across the sinkhole. "You're joking, right?"

"Trust me." Holding on to the fence, Callen shimmied to the adjacent enclosure and toward the smoldering mechanical area.

Krystal sighed, trailing behind him. "Easier said than done."

TWENTY-NINE

Garrett stood in the lobby with his jacket draped over his shoulders, watching the sky through the array of triangle-shaped windows. The sun hovered above the trees, surrounded by crystal blue. Irregular snowflakes fell and grazed the glass panels as the clouds above fought one last battle before being pushed away.

Garrett peered through the top of his shirt to check the bandage, then widened his stance and put both hands into his pants pockets. He seemed content in that moment, regardless of the haze building in the room and the carnage related to it waiting in the background.

He closed his eyes and pushed out a breath, counting down in his mind. When he reopened them, a black spot appeared on the horizon to the south.

"About damn time."

Before turning from the windows, he caught sight of a silhouette standing next to the entrance. He cocked his head and focused to determine if it was a trick of the light. Just as he moved forward for a better look, the glass in front of the silhouette shattered. Garrett recoiled from the sensation of being punched in the chest. His jaw dropped in a soundless scream, and he fell to one knee.

Crunching footsteps moved through fresh snow. Broken glass crashed to the ground, and the footsteps moved inside. Garrett held a shaking hand to shield his eyes and licked the corner of his top lip. "Nicely done."

Krystal leveled her aim between Garrett's eyes. "To be fair, I wasn't sure if it would work. With all your talk of technology and security, I figured it might have been bulletproof or something."

Garrett gave a cold smile. "Next time."

"Yeah, about that…"

The service door from the hallway snapped open, and Linford burst into the lobby with a gun in each hand. He snapped a quick glance at Garrett, then turned both guns on Krystal.

Krystal kept her focus. "Linford, listen to me." Her lips were the only part of her body to move. "He lied to us. He had no intention of letting any of us out of here."

"Bullshit."

Garrett winced. "Linford. Shoot her."

"He just wanted to clean up his mess. He killed Ellery and Johnathan. He tried to kill me too."

"No, he wouldn't—"

Garret slumped forward. "*Linford, goddamn it.*"

"I was with Callen. He forced both of us out into those cages. The explosion—"

Linford shuffled sideways toward the reception desk. "That was probably you."

Garret's face flushed, and spit flew from his lips as he screamed out. "*It was them. Shoot her.*"

"Linford. Stop."

All eyes turned to the broken window. Callen held a hand flat against the frame, then stepped into the lobby. "She's telling the truth."

"Don't listen to him. *They're lying.*"

Linford opened his mouth to speak, but the pleading look in Krystal's eyes halted his response.

Krystal took a step forward with her gun still trained on Garrett. "Johnathan and Ellery were locked in with the infected. He left them here to die, Linford. He left us all to die."

Linford let out a sharp breath and lowered his guns. He holstered one, then turned away, shaking his head. "Motherfucker."

"You useless piece of shit." Garrett took half a breath and groaned. "You're getting paid to do a job, *so fucking do it.*"

Linford's lips twisted into a frown. "Keep your fuckin' money. I've done some shady shit here, but this is too much."

Garrett lowered his head and screamed out. "*Fuck.*"

"Son of a bitch." Linford tightened his jaw and glared at Krystal. "Put that fuckin' thing down already. We need to get the fuck outta here."

Callen stepped forward. "Linford?"

"What, man?"

"You weren't in on it, were you?"

Linford's eyes narrowed, and he craned his neck. "'Scuse me?"

Callen clenched his hands at his sides. "I'm asking if you were in on his plan."

Linford scowled. "Fuck no."

Callen eyed him for a moment, letting his response sink

in, then looped a thumb under his empty holster. "Good. I don't want to have to take you out."

"Yeah, well, I'd appreciate it if you didn't." Linford focused on a dark corner of the room, away from Krystal and Garrett. Pushing his hat back on his head, he wiped at his brow. "The fuck did I get myself into here?"

Through the broken window, the pounding of helicopter blades called out in the distance.

Krystal lowered her weapon but kept it ready. "I need my rifle and my pack."

"Rifle's in lockup. Next to the office." Linford held out the key. "Here."

"No, you go. I'll follow."

Linford shrugged. "Whatever."

Krystal passed her gun to Callen. "Don't get too comfortable with it."

Callen nodded, took the gun, and aimed it at Garrett.

Wasting no time, Krystal stalked off toward the service hallway. Linford jumped in front of her and unlocked the door. He opened it a crack and pushed it near closed when lazy smoke began to flow around the door and into the lobby.

"We need to get in and get out. The fire's getting worse, and I think we might have a few friends to worry about as well."

"Are you serious?"

Linford glanced back to Garrett, still wheezing on the ground. "When I found him by the basement, he made it seem like you guys were up to something. Now, I'm thinkin' he might've done something stupid."

"Great."

Linford pushed through the door with one gun raised. Shuffling into the haze, he rushed around the corner to the office corridor. Krystal stayed close on his heels. The office door was still open, and a dim glow pushed out into the murky darkness. Linford stepped in to grab one of the lanterns, then moved to the door further along the wall and unlocked it. He propped open the gun cabinet, and stood to one side.

Krystal lifted her rifle and slid the strap over her shoulder. She scanned the rest of the cabinet. A neat line of guns hung from hooks on the left side, and stacks of ammunition lined the right. She stuffed her pockets full of clips, then took two handguns.

"Okay, let's go."

Linford led the way to the lobby. Krystal stopped at the doorway and looked back along the hall. The smoke grew dense, and the building echoed with unfamiliar noises. It could have been stress on the structure, damage from the explosion and fire, or it could have been something else. She followed Linford through the lobby door, but she planted her heel to stop it from latching.

Krystal walked up to Callen and held out her palm. "Gun."

Callen handed it over, and Krystal tucked it under the hem of her coat. She held out one of the handguns from the cabinet along with three clips.

"Thanks."

Krystal turned away without responding and moved to stand in front of Garrett.

Garrett propped himself against the lobby desk with one hand planted on the floor. His face was pale and his breath short. Old and new red stains soaked his shirt down to his pants.

Outside, the beat of helicopter blades overwhelmed the

still air. The machine eased down to the helipad, and the rotor calmed.

Krystal raised her voice as she motioned to the front door. "Linford, you should go check in with the pilot."

Linford nodded and headed toward the entrance.

"Hey."

He stopped and looked back.

Krystal pointed to Garrett. "He died in the explosion."

Linford's eyebrows pinched together.

"Got it?"

He nodded but averted his eyes, then strode out the door.

Linford met the pilot halfway. As they talked, the pilot looked around Linford to the shattered front glass and hint of smoke in the lobby. When the conversation concluded, the pilot hesitated but returned to the helicopter.

Linford came back through the front door.

"So?"

"I don't know if he bought all the way in, but he's getting ready to leave."

"Good. You guys should go."

"You're not coming?"

Krystal shook her head. "I need to get back to camp. I'll sort things out from there."

Linford shrugged. "If anyone can, I expect you'd be the one to do it."

"Hey, I still need to get my pack from upstairs." Krystal held out her hand.

"Sure, now you're okay going on your own." Linford took the key from his pocket and tossed it to Krystal. He picked up a bag from the long chaise, gave Garrett a brief glance, then looped around to the entrance. On his way, he nudged Callen with his elbow. "You coming?"

Callen did not respond at first.

Linford stopped. "Hey. Callen."

Callen slowly met Linford's gaze, and he shrugged. "Not sure that I'm ready to go back to civilization just yet."

Linford cocked his eyebrow. "Well, that I didn't expect." He checked his watch. "Just in case, you've got about two minutes to make up your mind."

Callen nodded.

Linford let out a deep breath, then turned to leave. "Take care, man."

As he watched Linford board the helicopter, Krystal came up beside Callen. "You know you're not coming with me, right?"

Callen's stern face broke into a weak smile. "Oh, I'm aware."

"Good." Krystal raised a hand to set it on his shoulder, but hesitated and lowered it. "I need to head upstairs quick."

"Yeah, go."

Krystal climbed the stairs two at a time. As she crested the top, a wave of heavy smoke pushed toward her. She held one arm across her face and crouched low, then advanced to the room where she had stayed the night before.

Inside, with the door closed, the air cleared. Krystal bolted around, collecting weapons from their hiding places. In the coatroom, she packed them away, along with the gun taken from the lockup, and donned the protective leather guards. Finishing with her pack, Krystal slipped it on and moved out into the wide hall. At the top of the stairs, she stopped and glanced back.

Focusing on the rooms where Ellery and Johnathan had slept, she contemplated checking for anything important they might have left behind. A fresh explosion shook the building's far end, and the glass surrounding the aviary cracked and fell. With the decision made for her, Krystal sprinted to the main level.

When she entered the lobby, her pace slowed. Garrett had not moved from his slumped position against the reception desk. Each sharp breath rattled deep in his chest. Callen stood in front of the broken window and watched as the helicopter's engine revved from a dull roar to a scream. The blades slashed the air and pulled the machine high into the sky. When it disappeared behind the trees, Callen faced into the lobby. He clenched his jaw, and his eyes focused on nothing in particular.

Krystal snapped her fingers. "Hey, you okay?"

Callen's eyes shifted to Krystal. He paused, then turned sideways and lifted the hem of his jacket and shirt.

Krystal's back straightened. "When did that happen?"

Callen pulled his hand away, letting the layers drop over the uneven scratches on his mid-section. "In the enclosure."

"Fuck."

"Yup."

"Wait. What about the vaccine? Are you telling me…"

Callen shrugged. "You know it doesn't work all the time. Especially with the amped-up shit they've been pumping into those people."

"Callen, I'm—"

Callen raised a hand. "Save it. I'm not dead yet."

Krystal nodded and lowered her eyes.

"Anyway. You heading south?"

"Yeah."

"I got a ride out of here. Could give you a lift if you want."

Krystal watched his eyes. "I appreciated it, but I'll be okay."

"Good." Callen forced a smile. "Figure I'm heading the other way anyhow."

Krystal returned the gesture. "Well, if you need it, the cabin is about five clicks south-southeast. You're welcome to use it if you need to get out of the elements. Just don't forget to clean up after yourself."

"I'll keep it in mind."

Krystal looked at the key in her hand. She bounced it once in her open palm, then dropped it to the floor. "Okay, we should go."

Behind them, Garrett coughed, and a trickle of blood ran down his lip. "I'm going to find you, both of you, and I'm going to make you disappear."

Krystal glanced at Garrett. "While part of me thinks I'd like to see you try, that's not going to happen." She waved her hand to the ceiling. "This right here, this will be your ending."

"I will never end." He turned his head to face her. "*This* will never end."

Krystal's face flushed as she scowled. She took one step toward Garrett with her fists clenched, but advanced no further. "Your opinion doesn't matter. Not anymore."

In the quiet, the soft turning of hinges sounded out like an alarm. Krystal eyed the entrance of the service hall. "Speaking of which."

Retrieving her gun from under her coat, she ran for the broken front window, then tucked and jumped through the ring of jagged glass. In the soft daylight, she paused to look back. Callen hopped out and veered off to the right side of the building. He stopped at the corner and faced the trees.

"Callen."

"Yeah?"

"Thank you."

Callen lowered his eyes and turned to go. "Yeah."

Krystal squinted at the lobby as bodies stormed the space. She spun on her heels and ran. The hammering of her boots in the snow was not enough to drown out the snarling and urgent need to do harm. Garrett shouted an indiscernible slur before his words escalated to panicked screaming and then fell into silence.

At the treeline, Krystal slid behind a thick trunk and knelt. She dropped her pack and rifle to the ground, then pulled out and raised her handgun toward the building. A face appeared in the broken window, bloodied and raw. The big man held a hand to his eyes, shielding the daylight. Krystal waited for him to turn around and retreat from the glare. Instead, he lowered his hand and moved through it.

"You've got to be shitting me."

With a twisted sneer on his face, the big man picked up speed. Steaming bodies poured from the hole behind him like angry hornets from a kicked nest. They charged fast, each intent on getting to Krystal first.

Krystal leaned in and took aim. With each squeeze of the trigger, one fell. The big man continued on, stepping over bodies as he went. She ejected an empty clip, reloaded, and fired four more rounds.

The big man's bare foot came down on the head of the last to fall. It eclipsed the strained face of a man with a newly formed hole at his temple. Pushing deep into the snow, his skull cracked under pressure as the big man charged.

Krystal's stance faltered as he neared. She fired two shots. The rounds sank into his shoulder and chest with no visible effect. She squeezed the trigger twice more. The first bullet broke through his cheekbone, and the hammer fell on an empty chamber with the second.

Raising his giant fists, the big man lunged forward, but she tucked and rolled away. Tripping on the open air, he stumbled to his hands and knees. Krystal was gone by the time he looked back.

She pushed herself into the clearing, searching her pockets for a fresh clip. She cursed herself for leaving the extra gun and ammo in her pack as she removed the last one from her jacket. After driving it home, she spun to face the treeline.

Now upright, the big man took long steps toward her, snow melting down his face, washing away blood and gore. A snowmobile broke out along the treeline, screaming forward at full throttle, and split the narrow space between the man and Krystal. Kicking a heavy boot out, the driver caught the big man in the stomach. He let out a gasp and collapsed to his knees.

Krystal capitalized on the opportunity and charged. Her last step sent her flying into the air, connecting the heel of her boot against the big man's nose. It flattened, and blood sprayed over his face. Krystal balanced on his chest as he fell, snarling while she emptied an entire clip into his face. Bits of flesh and skull sprayed out. His body went limp as the steaming mess sank deep into the snow.

Krystal hopped down from his chest and stepped away when the snowmobile circled back and slid to a halt.

Callen's hand dropped away from the throttle, and he gave Krystal an upward nod. "You good?"

Krystal sat in the snow with one knee raised and the other leg crossed in front of her. She let out a sharp breath. "Think so."

"Good." Callen let a sly grin break across his face, then

bared down on the throttle and leaned to his right. The snowmobile arced north and sped away.

Krystal dropped her head forward and sighed. "Well, shit."

She pulled herself up as the hum of the snowmobile faded into the horizon. Pausing to take stock of her surroundings, she checked for the break in the trees she had come through the day before. As she started to move toward it, deep shadows began to flow and shift. They soon took form, and a group of figures emerged into the light. At first, Krystal saw hunting gear, or maybe a uniform. She allowed a glimmer of hope that Clint had found her. As the group advanced, that hope disappeared.

The faces of the strangers were gaunt. Blood seeped from their eyes, and darkness oozed from their mouths. Steam rising from their skin faded as those in the lead moved into the sunlight.

Krystal looked past the encroaching mob to the spot where she left her pack, then back to the building and the thick smoke billowing from the broken window.

"Goddamn it."

Catching a hint of activity to the east, she pointed in the opposite direction and ran.

As Krystal passed into the treeline, the sounds of growling and heavy footsteps behind her eased. Looping south, she eyed the open space as she maneuvered through bushes and low branches. Losing track of any movement, she slowed and stopped close to a broad tree.

While she listened, she worked to calm her racing heart. The forest around her stayed quiet, so she crept on to the next tree and then the next, using the column of smoke rising from the building to keep her bearings.

After passing through a tight grouping of young birch trees, she knelt behind a jagged rock sticking out of the ground. Peering over it, she caught a glimpse of her pack, now surrounded by blood-stained tracks in the snow. Leaning against the rock, she released the clip from her gun. She dropped it beside her and patted her pockets, but they were empty.

"Can't catch one fuckin' break, can I?"

Her breath caught at the first sound of footfalls in the snow behind her. She peered around the rock to see a man in a blue uniform with a shaved head scanning the trees. Not police, as she first suspected, but a security guard or rent-a-cop. As she sank back, she spotted a woman in jeans and a baggy sweater with a halo of steam crowning her head moving in from her left. A growl came from her right, but the trees obscured who might have uttered it.

Krystal stuffed the useless gun into a pocket and zipped it shut. Searching in and around her vest, she freed two long blades and held them low at her sides.

"All right, fuckers, *let's go.*"

Thank you for reading!

Reviews are extremely important to indie authors. They help us hone our craft and find new readers. If you enjoyed this book, please consider sharing your thoughts on Amazon, Goodreads, or BookBub.

———

———

Also by Shane Kroetsch

This and That but Mostly the Other
Into the Storm (The Storm Series Book 1)
Surviving the Storm (The Storm Series Book 2)

ACKNOWLEDGMENTS

Life doesn't happen in a straight line. It comes with ups and downs. Sometimes it goes too fast, or it takes too long, and there will be unexpected detours along the way. If this is the reality of life, then why should writing a book be any different?

As I clickety-clack these words into the old computer box, it's been over six years since the idea for the Storm came to me. Just before Christmas 2014, the eastern coast of Canada and the US were preparing for the storm of the century. Over 5,000 flights were cancelled, and curfews put in place. It all seemed a bit strange, at least to me, so of course, my inner storyteller came up with some interesting ideas about what could be behind it. What stuck was a government cover-up, one with deadly consequences.

To that point, I had only written short fiction, but as the idea grew in my mind, I knew this one would be bigger. I dove in head-first because that's what I do. The thing is, I had a lot to learn, and this is where the road began to get bumpy. Shortly after starting the story, I got overwhelmed, which led to distraction, and I set it aside for longer than intended.

November is National Novel Writing Month (NaNoWriMo), and authors all over the world set a goal to write 50,000 words in 30 days. In 2015, I figured I'd participate in my own way and finish the first draft of *Surviving the Storm*. I fell short of the goal but did well enough. After the month-long writing sprint was over, I didn't expect the little break I took to turn into weeks without writing at all. So, once again, the story was set aside, and I focused on other things.

Somewhere along the line, I decided I wanted to self-publish. I'm impatient, and I don't like gatekeepers, so why not, right? The plan was to put out both a collection of short stories and *Surviving the Storm* before the end of 2018. While growing as a writer, I struggled to cultivate realistic expectations regarding how long it takes to complete certain tasks. Through the process of getting the books ready, I had an amazing first experience with an editor, but it also gave a clear indication of my skillset. That, combined with the previously mentioned unrealistic expectations, pushed the launch of Surviving further down the line.

My first book, *This and That but Mostly the Other,* was released early in 2019. It was such an exciting and terrifying time. Look at this thing I made! I was on top of the world. A whole new chapter in my life laid ahead of me, and so much good change was coming at the same time. The possibilities seemed endless. On my way out of a day job that was making me miserable, I roped my best friend into joining me on this out-of-control creative freight train. Wonder Twin powers, activate! I don't remember ever being so excited for the future.

The problem with being on top is, there's really only one place to go. Life got messy, but I managed to keep the creative freight train rolling and make slow progress on Surviving. Eventually, I got it to a place where I thought it was done and ready for the world.

Then, in August of 2019, I went to a prominent local writing conference. It was enlightening, to say the least. With the vast wealth of new information rolling around in my head, it became clear that Surviving wasn't done, not even close. I decided that The Storm made much more sense as a three-part series. I blew up the manuscript, making sweeping changes to the flow of the story and adding what would become a rather important character. I'm going to publish three books in one year! I'm unstoppable! Oh, wait. No, I'm not.

Writing a book is the easy part. Making it good isn't necessarily so. Going through seventeen rounds of edits isn't easy *or* fun, especially when one has an unnatural need for things to be perfect. I started *Into the Storm* soon after the conference. It came fast, whether from the stars aligning or my hard work from the previous few years paying off. It gave me a vessel to explore how shitty people are in real life and to shine a light on it. It's something I love to do. Don't judge me.

Later in the year, the weight of the workload I created for myself, along with the general stress of life, got to me. The week before Christmas, I put everything writing-related in a box and hid it in the closet. All of it. This was a scary time, both for me and those closest to me, but I needed a break. The good that came from it was that I learned how to slow down, if only a little. Sometimes, a detour leads you to where you need to be.

We put *Into the Storm* together in record time, and it was released in April of 2020. Because timing is everything, the first round of local COVID restrictions shut the world down the day after picking up my book about a zombie pandemic from the printer. After five months of learning how to not stand too close to other people or touch my own face, we released *Surviving the Storm*. Two books came out during a year that felt like ten, or not even a year at all. Having the extra time to do so, we focused on business and launched a webstore to offer our wonderful creations to the world. We built an amazing display for our first solo market, but it hasn't been used yet because strangers aren't allowed to be in the same space together, except when we are.

Very little about the last two years has been easy, but, in many ways, it has been rewarding. Working on being a better writer is essential for me. Focusing on being present in my life and taking care of myself is just as important, but I find it hard to make it a priority. I'm trying to do better, I promise.

Into the Storm showed me what the process of creating a proper work of fiction can look like. *Surviving the Storm* was a much different situation. It was disjointed and took years. Even though writing Surviving was the trial by fire, and the idea for Into came after, I was still very nervous about the final instalment, *Chasing the Storm*. I am happy to report that it came even faster. It's the cleanest first draft I've ever written. It showed me how much progress I've made and makes me excited for the future. I'm getting closer to working at a sustainable pace. I realized things take longer in real life than they do in my head, and I've learned how to be okay with shifting deadlines.

In the end, I'm proud of this book. It's a feeling I haven't known to this extent before. I'm proud of my partner Kaleigh, how she's embraced this crazy dream and her own creativity. As good as I think *Chasing the Storm* is, along with the complete series overall, I know we're only getting better. Hold onto your hats, this freight train is just getting started.

To date, Shane has released a collection of short fiction, a zombie outbreak trilogy, and been featured in a growing number of anthologies. In his spare time, he builds projects out of old junk, paints watercolor blanket ghosts, and shakes his butt while the vinyl spins.